Double Dyno

By Sharon K Angelici

Prequel to
Yule be Home for Solstice
An Alice and Violet Story

Write with Light Publications Colorado, USA

ISBN: 9798884262928
ISBN: 9781970289046
Library of Congress Number: 2024934519

Dedication

David, Victoria and Davie, you inspire my storytelling and your support means everything to me.

Rach and Roz, you are my creative co-conspirators. Your skills make it possible for the rest of the world to read this story and I'm honored to share this earth with humans like you.

Michelle, Isa, Peg and Paula, an author could not ask for a more enthusiastic and supportive cheer squad. Thank you for always showing up for me.

Hill, you wonderful, creative being of light. Thank you for the late night moments. I cherish every one.

Kathy, thank you for Write With Light and for all the support as we publish my eleventh book together.

Jimmy, you big jerk. Wherever you are, I hope they have ethereal manuscript delivery. You should be here for the prequel but also know that I am writing more than I talk about writing.

Dad, thanks for reading the stories I write.

Mom, I wish you were here for every book I've published in the six years you've been gone. You would have loved Wildwood and Shay, Morgan and Ella, and I think you'd have liked Violet and Alice too. They're all a part of my queer little heart. A heart I wish you'd have known.

Prologue

"It's a long way down." Al clenched her hand tightly around the anchoring cable. The eighteen-strand twisted steel secured the bridge to the rock face she was dangling from. She was climbing, finally, or so she thought after hours of paperwork and detailed safety checks. As she looked over and out across the forest treetops beneath her, she could see a future for herself.

"Get back." The instructor tugged Al's shoulder, pulling the eighteen year old onto the slats of wood. "Girl, that's more than a long way down. You'll have a heart attack before you hit the ground."

"That's bullshit," Britt said as she leaned further, absolutely disconnected from the reality she was in. The permit clipped to her backpack gave her and Al twenty-four hours to navigate this hike through the rainforest. The clock was ticking but they didn't care. They wanted to see the tapered surface of the cliff their walkway was anchored to.

With her fingertip, Al flicked the bolt that seemed to defy science while tying the bridge to the cliffside. Her fingers were wrapped with a criss-crossing of tape, worn like a second skin to put protection between herself and the cracks she was about to wedge them into.

"It's not bullshit," the instructor said. "Your body will recognize it's falling and your heart will explode in your chest."

Britt didn't believe a word the guide was saying. If that was the body's reaction to falling, and you had to fall to make it happen, how would anyone report back what was happening? They'd already be dead. Distracted by this logic problem, Britt didn't recognize the narrowness of her next foothold and she slipped.

"Pay attention," the guide yelled as he tugged Britt onto the perch once again.

"I can't. It's all so beautiful." Britt's right arm locked at the elbow as she twisted her hips to pivot on the foothold. It was a climber's move. She'd practiced in the gym since she was eleven. Seven years of dangling from her toes and fingertips also gave her the ability to release her left hand as she turned to admire the view.

"It won't be so beautiful when they have to hose your brains off the rocks below us," the guide said.

Britt rapped her knuckles against the surface of the climbing helmet. "Brain's good."

"That's up for debate," Al said. "Get serious, will you?"

"Fuck off, Al." Britt locked her feet onto the foothold and pretended to throw a punch at her friend.

"I will not. I'm tied to this wall." Al toed the pinch, moving away from her friend and climbing partner.

The guide laughed. "If you're done screwing off, can we get to the test?"

Britt gave a left-handed salute. "Yes, captain."

Al held up a thumb. "Let's get to the ledge."

The next twenty minutes involved extended holds and exacting fingertips as they made their way across the face of the rock. It wasn't a difficult climb but it had specific intentions. Al and Britt were two of the three women determined to teach the skills they were exercising today and everything they were doing, good or bad, would determine if they made next level certifications.

In Al's mind, this was a formality. From the time she could walk, all she wanted to do was climb. To some people she encountered, this confidence came off as cocky.

The instructor watched them, impressed by the way they moved up and horizontally, clipping in and adjusting ropes to protect one another but also so casual that they could have been a meter off the ground in a climbing gym.

"How do you feel?" Al asked her friend.

Britt anchored her toes, her body seemingly defying the laws of physics as she leaned into the harness around her hips. "I feel like I'm invincible."

"Yeah, I feel it too." Al's smile filled the chiseled features of her face, making her look like the free spirit she was when her fingers held her above ground. There was no place they'd rather be.

"Can we do this forever?" Britt asked as her toe planted on the pinch.

"Not if you don't pass my test," the guide yelled.

"Right," they said in unison as Al reached the last anchored carabiner and hooked in.

"You're too cocky," he said.

Al didn't respond as she wrapped her fingers over the ledge and pulled her body up to stand on top. The view was more than breathtaking—it was a glimpse at what was to come, and Al felt it in her core.

"Not bad, eh?" Britt was seconds behind her friend and had to stretch to lop her arm over Al's six-foot frame.

"I think I'm in love." Al didn't look away from the landscape as her brain processed the view. The tips of the trees looked like a lush green carpet. She wanted to step off and walk across.

"Yeah, me too."

"Part one is a pass," the instructor said. "Take ten and we'll move on to the next exam." He scribbled in his notebook before tucking it into a zippered shirt pocket.

Al untied and sat down. As her feet dangled off the ledge, she sighed. "I don't ever want to be tied to an office chair."

Britt sat beside her, mirroring her best friend's position. She took off her helmet and tousled the sweat from her chin-length brown hair. "Isn't that the point of certifications: so we don't have to ever sit in chairs?"

Al removed her own helmet, releasing the shoulder-length dark hair partially bleached by the sun. "If we do it right, we can go anywhere in the world and climb everything we want."

Britt leaned against her best friend. "I wish Stacey was here."

"She'll be on the next one." Al kicked her feet up toward her chest, taking her friend's full weight against her. "If I had Stacey's family, I'd want to spend holidays at home, too."

"It's not easy being us."

Al snickered. "It sure isn't."

They sat in silence, enjoying the view and dreaming the dreams of their future.

"If you're finished, let's move on to the belaying exercises," the instructor said without pausing as he entered the path behind them. This was how the next twenty-four hours would go.

They'd listen to every instruction, take what was new, add it to their experience and move forward.

"Let's tie in." He tossed two different harnesses on the ground at Britt's feet.

"Race ya." Britt picked up a harness and tossed it to Al.

"It's not a competition." Al whispered. "This isn't the time." She looked pointedly at their instructor.

"Right." Britt stepped into the leg loops. "Too big." She handed the harness to Al.

"You're such an asshole." Al swapped the harness. It was true, Al had thick thighs and straight hips. She wasn't shy about the power in her body but she was also intent on balance for agility. With her long frame and lean shoulders, she was built to climb.

"Let me see your eights again," the instructor said as he handed each of them an end of rope. It wasn't attached to anything, which was perfect for the test.

Al gripped the end of the rope, stretching it across her chest. She whipped her wrist to make two turns on a loop and tucked the loose end through. Before she could count to ten, she was holding a perfect figure-eight knot in her hand. Britt finished hers a second later.

"I could do that blindfolded," Britt said.

"I don't want to know about you and blindfolds," Al joked as she passed her rope to the instructor.

He rolled it over to inspect each side. "Perfect."

"Thank you," Al said and stepped aside so he could inspect Britt's.

"Yours is equally good." The instructor kept both samples. "The wall is open. You've got twenty minutes to build your belay and get a teammate to the top."

They walked toward the cliff face. Although they liked the challenge of nature's climbing surfaces, Al and Britt spent most of their downtime practicing on artificial structures.

"Twenty minutes for this?" Britt looked up. "I can do this in five."

"*We* can do it in twenty, as a team." Al grabbed the end of the rope and tossed it to her friend. "You remember the team, right?'

"I remember." Britt said. "There's no one I'd rather have by my side than PB."

Al laughed. "You're such a smartass."

Britt was serious when she added, "You know I'm joking, right?"

"Mm hmm," Al mumbled.

"No, really. You are the best of us."

Al's smile grew. "Yep, I know, and that's why you'll climb, and I'll belay."

"Hilarious and boss-y," Britt joked as she skipped her way back to the climbing ledge, tied in and dropped off to lower herself down.

"It's called leadership. It's what we're here for," Al yelled and their instructor scribbled in the notebook as he focused his attention on Al.

Al ran her hands along the cracks in the mountainside, finding places to secure the anchoring cams. Fanning the gear on her harness to find the perfect fit was easy for her. It took less than a minute to anchor three points, attach her big two-forty sling and build her belay.

She stretched her arm out, measured a length across her chest and whipped a perfect figure-eight knot to tie in. Her technique was impressive as she looped the clove hitch locking her in the ready position. She moved to the edge and dropped the rope to the ground thirty-feet below.

"On belay," Al yelled. "Climb when ready." She waited a second and another for her climber to respond.

"Climber on," Britt yelled after tying in.

Al took up the slack as she sat on the ledge, her hands holding tight, one passing over the other but never losing grip on the rope. Brit was a skilled climber, talented and almost as fearless as Al. In the end, Britt was at the top in ten minutes.

"What took you so long?" Al joked as she pulled the slack up to the pooling pile of rope on the rock beside her.

"I don't know." Britt paused to look at the belay Al constructed. "I was waiting on you and your three-point better-safe-than-sorry belay build."

"That better-safe-than-sorry belay is exactly why she passed this test and earned her certification to guide." The instructor tugged a page from his notebook. "The papers will arrive in less than a week. I'll mail them tonight."

"Hell yeah!" Britt held up a hand for a high five before realizing the instructor hadn't mentioned her. "What about my papers?"

Al slapped her hand. "Dummy, we're a team."

He laughed at the two of them. "She's correct. A team application means a team certification."

"Double hell yeah!"

Al slapped the high five again. "We're actually going to do this."

"Hell yes we are!" Britt laughed. "Rack your sling and let's go celebrate."

Chapter One

"We're actually going to do this?" Al asked as she pulled her hand through her hair, lumping it into a pile on her head with an elastic band.

"It's been ten years." Britt chuckled. "You've pined over this for ten damn years."

"So what? The manufacturer is pretty supportive of our community." Al's adoration of the car company was practical but also emotional, and she felt excited as she sat on the ground thumbing through the pages. "Not a lot of people are."

It was their last night in the woods. The two of them were sleeping under the stars, the smell of campfire and juniper lingering in the air. The place was a little slice of heaven neither was eager to escape.

"I know that not a lot of people are supportive, duh, but…"

Al interrupted, "It's fine. Stay focused. We're shopping for one of the biggest things of my life." She turned the page. "Will you, please?" She leaned in for more light from the campfire.

"Oh yeah, baby!" Britt pressed her calloused hands to the page, squeezing closer for a better view. "That's the one right there. Damn, it's so hot, Al."

"I don't know, Britt." Al ran a calloused finger across the picture. Her hands were larger by almost half and equally as strong. Climber's hands, a girl said once in a bar. She didn't mind the comment because as gnarly as they were, they were also the tools of her trade.

"Come on, Al, you didn't like that one because 'it wasn't perfect.'" Britt's fingers formed quotation marks. Exhausted by the supportive-friend role, she cut the unspoken opinions tumbling around in her head. She turned another page, slicing her thumb on the edge in the process. "Shit, that's it. I'm so over trying to find the perfect yin to your yang in a glossy pamphlet."

Britt walked across their campsite to the basin balancing in the middle of their makeshift log table. Britt, in all of her five-foot-six height, swished her hand through what was left of their wash water.

"Come on, it's a paper cut." Al leaned closer to the light from the fire.

"A paper cut from trying to find the next love of your life," Britt spat out in frustration.

"Maybe I want something better than what I've settled for since high school." Al turned the page, her breath catching when she saw the image. "Oh, yeah baby." She held the picture for Britt to see. "She's definitely the one."

"Why that one?" Britt asked, grabbing the page and flipping back and forth from the previous options. "They're all the same."

"No way. This one is my girl," Al slapped the image with the back of her hand. "Tomorrow we'll hike out of here and go find her."

Britt unzipped her tent. "You're going to dream about her all night, aren't you?"

"I might." Al kicked her long legs out in front of her; finally free from her socks and shoes, she wriggled her toes.

"Gross," Britt said through the zippering sound of the tent's mesh screen. "You need to find a woman."

~~~~~~~~~~

"Am I allowed to touch her?" Britt asked as her bandaid-covered fingertip hovered over Al's new love.

"You, but only you." Al stood beside Britt, leading her around the sleek curves of the body.

Their hike from the remote camping spot was the fastest pace Al had ever set and Britt felt the challenge to keep up with her friend's long-legged strides. There was time for a shower at the truck stop, a quick change into clean clothes and the two of them landed where they were now.

Britt turned in a little circle. "Who else is here to touch her?"

Al found it comical to watch her best friend twirl around. "Right," she said dismissively, squatting low for a closer look.
~~~~~~~~~~

"You're a little tall for her, don't you think?" Britt laughed at her own joke. She couldn't wait to see her best friend pretzel-twisting to sit inside.

Al stood to her full height, measuring herself beside her friend. "I'm a perfect fit for her. Don't you worry, this is going to be a lifetime commitment."

"You know, they say red makes it go faster." Britt punched Al's shoulder.

Al squatted to the ground, rubbing dust from the car's rim. "You and your redheads."

"No apologies." Britt gave a ridiculously toothy grin.

"Don't say it." Al held up a silencing finger.

"Oh but you know, chicks dig red."

"Ugh." Al shook her head.

"Would you like to take it for a test drive?" the dealer asked, dangling the keys in front of them. Distracted by their bantering, they hadn't heard the dealer return with a set of keys.

"Her," Al corrected him.

"Apologies." He cleared his throat. "Would you like to take her—"

Al snatched the keys from his hand. "Hell yes I would, and you see that car over there?" She pointed to the tan Escort parked in the customer lot.

He nodded.

"She's the trade. Make it a good one." Al ducked her head as she sat behind the steering wheel. The dashboard was sleek and the stereo had both a cassette and CD player. Al turned the key and the hum of the engine was like a kitten's purr.

She shifted the car into reverse and backed halfway through the lot before turning around to drive out onto the highway.

"She's amazing." Britt rubbed the dashboard.

"I know." Al drove down a county road, pushing the accelerator hard to the floor. "It feels so adult to sit in a new car."

Britt laughed. "You're the only adult I know."

"Yeah, I know. I've seen your friend group."

"Hey." Britt leaned away. "Not nice."

"You just said I'm the only adult you know?"

Britt could hear the annoyance in her friend's tone. "Let's be real. You've been an adult since you were eleven."

"Out of necessity." Al said as her hands shuffled across the steering wheel to make a turn. "Survival of the fittest."

"Exactly my point." Britt reached to turn the radio on and Al pushed her hand away. "Can you even afford twenty thousand dollars for a car?" Britt asked as she raised and lowered the windows instead.

"I've got most of the cash from the last trip," Al glanced quickly at her friend, "and with this next one I'll be able to put down close to twenty thousand, so I'm going to borrow from my savings, temporarily. At zero-percent interest I'm almost stealing this car from them." She stopped in a vacant parking lot.

"Trading in the old beater might get you a couple thousand, too." Britt gripped the safety handle above the passenger seat window as Al reversed the car, swooping and swerving to test the steering.

"I'm not holding my breath for more than three grand, but I'm driving this baby off the lot today." Al hit the brakes hard. "Fuck! I love this car!" She drummed her hands on the steering wheel.

"You're going to make me puke." Britt covered her mouth.

Al used the button on the door to roll Britt's window all the way down. "Don't puke inside her." She giggled and shifted the car into drive. "That's not how I want to break her in."

~~~~~~~~~~~

"With the title and your new license plates, the fees total seventy-nine dollars." The cashier at the dealership window handed Al the forms for her signature.

"Great." Al signed the documents and paid the fee with cash.

"Your plates and tags." The cashier passed them across the desk. "If you need help we can put them on for you."

"We've got it. We're going to take a picture when we do it," Britt interrupted, waving her polaroid camera. "Plus, my girl doesn't need any help with tools."

Al pushed her friend as they turned to leave. Once they were outside, she bumped her hip. "I don't need help with tools. What kind of lame-ass line is that?"

"It wasn't a lame-ass line, Al. It was a genuine revelation of truth. We are independent chicks. We don't need someone to turn a screwdriver for us." Britt held out a hand for a fist bump and Al pushed it aside.
~~~~~~~~~~~

The Subaru Outback was parked in front of the dealership. While Al signed her life away, the salesman ran it through a car wash. The shine made Al stop to admire her purchase. "She's a real beaut."

"You're a lucky bitch." Britt brushed at a bead of water on the hood,

Al unwrapped the license plates. "Yeah, right now I kinda feel like I am."

"One M B three five S," Britt grabbed Al's wrist so she could read the numbers and letters. "Holy shit, that's so great."

Al raised a questioning eyebrow. "What's so great?"

"They named her."

Al pressed the expiration stickers to the plate she was about to attach to the rear of the car. "What are you talking about?" She set the plates on the ground while she opened the multi tool she carried in her pocket. With a knee resting on the ground, she removed the anchoring bolts.

"Read the plate, you big dummy."

Al stood, twirling her dark curly hair into a top-head bun and fastening it with the elastic from her wrist. "What the hell are you talking about? Read what?"

"The plate. It says 'One M B three five S'." Britt spelled it out.

Al clapped. "Congratulations, kindergartener, you know your letters and numbers."

Britt bumped her friend on the hip. "No, smart ass. The number 'one' and an 'M' spells 'I'm'. 'B-three-five-S' spells 'Bess'. I'm Bess."

Al squatted behind the vehicle. As she screwed the plate to the car, she connected with Britt's observation. "That's—"

"Fucking awesome!" Britt said, pumping her arms and grinning widely.

"Yeah, it kinda is," Al agreed.

Chapter Two

"This car is so great." Britt rubbed her head, finger combing the tangles from her hair before pulling on the EAG logo ball cap. The hat and their polo shirts were recent additions to their professional team apparel for the Extreme Adventure Group, their dreams manifested behind the three scrolled letters worn with pride.

Al was excited to lead the week-long trip with Bess as their new ride. It would be the first of many trips, she thought. "I know she's the perfect addition to the team. The hiking gear fits so much better in the back and we have enough space to pick up PB, too."

"This is going to be our best guide-vehicle ever." Britt drummed the dashboard with both hands, beating harder than Al liked.

"Hey, hey!" Al yelled. "Be nice to my girl Bess."

Britt adjusted her drumming motion to adore the Outback with the most loving caress. "Sorry, baby. I cherish you like the wonderful new love of Al's life that you are."

Al chuckled. "That's better. Maybe a little over the top, but much better." She turned the car into the campground, heading to the designated spot for EAG's guides.

"There she is." Britt rolled the window down and screamed at their friend, "Jam Girl!" The greeting was loud and ridiculously exaggerated, which was exactly how the two related to one another.

Al shook her head as she noticed the two-quart glass canning jar on the ground beside the bulging backpack. Stacey had an insatiable addiction to homemade sweet preserves, an appreciation handed down from her gran.
She sampled berries everywhere they went, making her the team expert when it came to life-saving survival foraging. Britt called

her Jam Girl, but Al chose PB instead. Peanut butter went best with jelly, always. What made the nicknames more entertaining was that Stacey didn't care for either of them in the beginning.

The wolf-whistle coming from PB's mouth was slow and outrageously over-the-top. As Al pulled closer, PB wasn't shy about admiring the Outback, from the star-sign emblem on the hood to the sparkling license plate on the rear bumper. In her adoring state, she nearly tripped over her backpack as Al came to a stop.

"She's fucking gorgeous!" PB trailed her finger over the pinstripe along the side.

"You should have been with us at the dealership," Britt said. "Al got such a sweet deal and they gave her a thousand dollars more than expected for the clunker."

"Really?" PB asked as she tugged the door handle.

"Practically stole it off the lot," Britt bragged.

"It's all that bossiness." PB opened the passenger door and popped her head inside. "Ooh, it's so luxurious, and I don't have to ride in the back with all of the gear."

The split backseat was folded down halfway, leaving plenty of room for the smallest member of their team to ride in comfort.

"No more steerage seating for you," Al joked, rubbing her side as she twisted around to look at her back seat.

"A lady could get some action in here." PB leaned out to grab her backpack.

"A lady would need to find a lady first." Britt laughed.

"Can it, you're single too." Al rolled the window up, favoring the muscle tightness as she adjusted in her seat.

"By choice." Britt pretended to be serious for a few seconds before all three of them broke out in laughter. They weren't single by choice, unless prioritizing EAG was understood as a life commitment, lending toward 'one-night and done' relationships.

"Who has time for love when you're on the road twenty-four seven?" Al's question was mostly rhetorical.

"Yeah, not a ton of available choices," PB joked.

"I do alright," Britt said, and she spun around to point at her friend. "And before you make a shitty comment about my bisexuality, remember I won't find it funny."

"I'm not saying a word." PB held up her hands defensively.

"Good, keep it that way." Britt turned toward Al. "And you?"

"It's hard enough in the outside world. I'm not bringing any of that in here. Anyway we have Bess and we need to celebrate her!"

"Yes, let's celebrate our new family car," Britt said. She unscrewed the lid on the canteen.

"Family, I like that," PB said as she relaxed against the soft seats. "So if we're family, who's calling who 'Daddy'?"

Britt spit her water on the dash and Al swerved toward the ditch, slamming the car to a stop.

"You—stop it!" Al pointed at PB. She turned to Britt. "And you better be drinking water."

Britt gripped the cuff of her sweatshirt sleeve and wiped the dashboard. "It's only water. I promise."

"Good." Al looked at PB in the rearview mirror. "Behave."

PB giggled. "So you're definitely not the mom."

"Bossy big sister is more like it," Britt teased.

"I'm the boss of you." Al chuckled as she pointed between the two. "That's all you really need to know right now." She tipped her head toward Britt. "Why don't you two review my notes for this trip?"

Al touched the clipboards wedged between Britt's seat and the center console. Britt passed one to PB, and they were serious for the next few minutes as they read through the printed materials Al had attached to the clipboard.

"We have six clients on this one." Britt said, flipping between the pictures and notes . Reviewing clients and their pre-trip skill level was a crucial part of their preparations. Like a self-control switch had been flipped, the group transformed from their screw-around best friend comfort zone into the focused leaders guiding life-changing experiences.

"Two men and four women." Al had the clients' histories memorized.

"This is a great group size. They'll all get one-on-one time. Any experience between them?" PB asked.

"The guys have finished a few fourteeners," Al said, "and all four of the women are looking for the next level."

"Next level," PB chuckled. "Fifty bucks two of them show up in shiny new hiking boots."

"With zero water reserves," Britt added.

"Hey, no one comes out here with skill and experience the first time. It's learned." Al looked in the rearview mirror. "Remember, we're the teachers."

"Yes, Mom," they said in unison.

"Never gonna be the mom, but I am your team leader. Let's make this a great trip for all of them." Al turned into the entrance to the state park, driving slowly as they approached the gate so the ranger could check for their annual pass and wave them through.

When they arrived at site sixteen, PB was the first to point out their clients for the trip. The group of six had congregated near a picnic table with their gear piled on top.

"I see so many shiny boots over there." Britt turned around to fist bump PB. "You better add two more Moleskin blister packs to the first-aid kit."

"Already doing it." PB's shoulders shook as she fought to hide her laughter.

"Get it together before we go out there and meet them." Al didn't show emotion for or against the attire their clients wore. They'd find out soon enough that the best time for new boots wasn't day one of a hike.

"What's up with your side?" Britt asked.

"It's nothing," Al said.

"It's something."

"Later," Al tipped her head toward the waiting clients. "It can wait."

~~~~~~~~~~~

"Lose her number." The hiker's phone number was printed in marker with tiny hearts dotting the I's. Al leaned over Britt's shoulder to snatch the paper from her friend. "This woman's too adorable for you."

"Come on, Al." Britt pulled her hands away, somehow extending beyond Al's ridiculously long arm span.

"Rules are rules." PB spun round and round on the bar stool like a child on a carousel, plucking the crumpled paper from the two of them.

"You're just saying that because I got her number and you didn't."
~~~~~~~~~~~

"Absolutely, hell yes I am." PB kicked a boot-covered foot off the bar to spin her chair around again, flapping the phone number like an Olympic ribbon dancer.

"Knock it off, both of you. Let's start going over the yeas and nays from this last trip." Al grabbed the back of PB's spinning chair. "And stop making me dizzy, will ya?"

"Always so serious, boss." Britt picked up her drink, taking a long, deliberately slurpy sip.

"Never, ever serious," Al said as she tossed the folder on the table.

"You get me at one hundred percent when we guide, so I get to screw off as much as I want when I'm not," Britt said.

"Duly noted." Al chuckled as she opened the folder for Britt's adorable phone number lady. "Kennedy Miller, aka lose-her-number lady."

"I'd take her again," Britt said.

"I'm not counting your obviously unbiased opinion."

PB interrupted. "Miller took our suggestions well. I think she picked up new skills fast. She was definitely the top of this class."

Al made a note in the margin before pointing her pen at Britt. "See, constructive criticism."

"Yeah, but not necessarily a top." Britt sipped again, anticipating the slap to the shoulder that came. "Ow. With or without getting a phone number, I'd take her again."

"Get your horny head out of the gutter, Britt." Al flipped the folder over. "Philomena Jardan?"

"Yep." PB waved at the waitress, drawing a circle in the air for a round of drinks. "Totally number two in that group."

"I agree, even if she's straight," Britt added.

Al shook her head. It was going to be a long debriefing if Britt didn't let up on objictifying their clients. She shuffled two folders to the top of the pile. "Let's talk about Steven and Kris."

"Yes, the dudes." PB emptied her glass.

"They are definitely experienced, but not cocky about it. Nice for a change," Britt shared.

PB wrinkled her nose. "It was refreshing to not have my ten years of technique and skill explained away." When PB spoke of experience, she wasn't shy. She, like the rest of the team, had practically been climbing since birth. What one of them lacked in skill, the other had, and that was the strength of EAG.

Love and respect for nature was PB's lifeblood. It could have been her Indigenous roots, and her belief that she was connected to the soul of the earth.

"Ah, yes. It's always refreshing to not deal with fragile egos." Al made notes in their files. The day progressed as they finished the least exciting part of their business.

"Yeah, some guys can be scary," Britt said.

"They sure can," Al agreed.

"Oh, shit." PB looked at Britt. "Speaking of scary guys… we didn't tell you about Al's dude fight on the bus."

"Dude fight?" Britt asked.

"Yeah, on the way to get the car before you got Bess."

"Please don't," Al closed the folders and tucked the files into her backpack. "My ribs still hurt."

"What dude? What bus?" Britt was more than curious. It wasn't like Al to get caught up in any kind of fight, especially one involving a random guy.

"You're gonna laugh; it's insane. So we're coming back from that skill-building thing in the middle of—I don't even remember where." PB waved off the thought.

"Missouri," Al corrected. "It was Missouri."

"Whatever. We were in the sticks and your fearless leader over there hadn't showered for days."

"Water was scarce on this one," Al explained. "You were stinky, too."

"Maybe, but you were bad." PB fanned the air. "So we get on this bus and seat ourselves away from the rest of the passengers because she reeks."

"We get it." Al raised her middle finger. "I should have sponged off."

"At the very least." PB pinched her nose.

"So what happened?" Britt flapped her hand to move the story along.

"Nothing happened at first. Al and I slept, mostly, but then this guy got on at a remote pick-up point. You know those stops where the serial killers get on?"

"Shut the hell up." Britt gasped and Al shook her head.

"Okay, so we're alive and he's not a serial killer," PB conceded. "Now remember, there are like thirty other empty seats on the bus and this guy sits right in front of us."

"Not because he liked the back of the bus," Al added.

"Right." PB grinned. "Not even five minutes goes by before the dude proceeds to pull out a knife."

"Wait, what?" Britt asked, confused.

"High as a kite, I shit you not." PB's arms waved wildly as she spoke. "I'm not sure what he was on but his eyes were bulging and his pupils were black holes. He thought he could rob us like that." She pointed at Al. "So stinky over here leaps over the seat, full steam ahead, and decks the dude solid to the face."

"Fuck yeah! That's our butch-ass prize fighter." Britt held up her hand for a high five and PB slapped it.

"Yeah, a big fucking hero," Al said. "Two things happened and neither of them were good."

"What happened?" Britt asked, leaning forward.

PB chuckled. "When her fist hit him, the dude crumpled like an accordion," she smashed her palms together, "and the bus driver slammed on his brakes so hard that Al ended up five rows forward with two bruised ribs."

"No shit?"

"No shit." Al shook her head. "The driver was such a dick. He didn't move an inch until the cops came. All three of us were taken off the bus and handcuffed for bullshit assault because the driver only saw me hit the dude."

"You got a rap sheet now, convict?" Britt joked.

"Nah, you know her." PB hitched her thumb at Al. "She sweet-talked the cop, really played up the rib thing, and when they found the dude's knife they had to let us go."

"Yeah, in the middle of nowhere, because they wouldn't let us back on the bus."

"What did you do?" Britt asked.

"We did what we do best." Al polished her knuckles on her shirt.

"You rented a car?" Britt guessed.

"Well, yes, eventually. But first we hiked our asses to the nearest town," PB added. "We had to pool our funds for the rental car and damn near broke the cash bank."

"Holy shit, what a story," Britt said.

"Oh yes," Al said. "If I never ride a bus again it'll be too soon."

Chapter Three

"Hey, best friend," Britt yelled from the curb outside the backpacker's hostel. She shrugged the backpack off her shoulder as the red Outback's window rolled down.

Al pulled Bess to a stop and hit the unlock button. "What's up?"

"Sold my old clunker, and guess what I got for your new girlfriend?" She fanned a fistful of cash at Al.

"Are you serious?" Al asked. "You've been trying to sell that thing since I bought Bess six months ago."

Britt leaned over to look at the car's odometer. "Look at us putting eighteen-thousand miles on her."

Al ran her hands across the steering wheel. "She's so great. Still has that new car smell."

"Well she's about to have a new roof-rack look, too." Britt tucked the cash inside the glove box.

"Just in time for the next trip." Al put the car into drive. "I guess we're stopping at the dealership before we get PB?"

"Yep, that's why you're picking me up now." Britt smiled. "Bess is getting some new frills—it's on me and the beater."

It took less than two hours for the dealership to install the roof-rack system and give Bess a wash. Al wasn't over the joy of new car ownership yet, which was obvious as her chest puffed a little when the car came out of the dealership's carwash.

"Will you look at her?" Britt whistled.

"Best decision I ever made." Al took the keys from the mechanic.

"Do you want me to explain the features of this roof-rack system?" he asked.

"Seriously?" Britt's hip jutted and her arms crossed over her chest as she positioned herself in her most intimidating warrior-like position. "The two of us have done extensive research on this and we know every single feature."

"You know about the bike rack?"

"We know how to adjust the crossbars, too," Britt answered before Al could.

"Sounds like you know."

Britt opened the passenger door. "We do."

Al leaned against the roof of the car, talking to the mechanic with the Outback between them. "Thanks for the help and for shining my girl up."

"No problem," he said before returning to the garage.

"Dickhead." Britt chuckled. "Like we are a couple of helpless little girls."

Al was also slightly irritated. "I'm pretty sure he doesn't think that anymore." She pushed the cassette into the player and the music turned up higher than she anticipated.

Britt yelled, "Kinda loud, isn't it?"

"If it's too loud, you're too old," Al joked as she lowered the volume.

"Very funny." Britt adjusted the seat to lean back and closed her eyes. "Let me know when we're there."

"Okay, Grandma." Before Britt could respond, Al raised the volume a little higher.

~~~~~~~~~~~

A few weeks later, Al sat half in and half out of Bess at a gas station while she watched the numbers grow on the pump. This month, they were taking a break in the Pacific Northwest, and the mountain view through the windshield was spectacular. Twenty minutes later, she navigated the intersection heading into the national forest.

Life was good and so was the future of their business. Today was climbing-readiness day; what she liked least and most about their new client protocols. To keep insurance premiums affordable, and for team safety, they'd established this testing day to weed out customers who might not be ready for their next-level adventures.

They were not hiking guides—they were Extreme Adventure Group, leaders of tough hikes. If you made it through their tests,
~~~~~~~~~~~

you might make it through the two-week trip that was an escape from modern living.

She turned off the music as she pulled into the parking space in front of the high-ropes course entrance. Britt was already at the top, tied in tightly to the repelling tower. Al knew what was coming next as she watched her friend fall backward, drop more than halfway down and stop. Al heard screams from the person standing on the ground. Their long curly hair puffed out around the helmet they wore. Britt was trying to impress them, which could only mean the person under the helmet had caught Britt's interest.

Al rolled the window down. "Hey, hot shot!" she yelled, and Britt let go with one hand to wave like a princess in her carriage.

"Al is here! Now we can start this party!" PB said. She was standing on the ground beside a few of their potential clients. If Al had read the situation correctly, she was certain this party had started without her.

"How's everyone this morning?" Al asked as she approached the group. She recognized one of the clients, Greta, from a park meet-and-greet earlier that week but the curly-haired person was a yet-to-be-evaluated and recently registered client.

"So far, this morning, we're great. I was showing Violet the ropes." Britt whipped the belay rope attached to her climbing harness. PB gave it a pull, yanking Britt off her feet.

"That's great." Al put out her hand to greet Violet who was almost a foot shorter. "Welcome to Extreme Adventure Group's test day. I'm Al Hadley."

"Oh." Violet hesitated, her confusion clear, as she said, "You're not a guy." Violet noticed a few additional things about the taller woman, the most visceral being her chiseled chin and her obviously muscular shoulders.

The scene was awkward for the onlooking group as Al held out a hand but Violet didn't shake it.

"Al is short for Alice," Britt explained to the now silent woman. "She is definitely not a guy."

"You're an all-women's outdoor group?" Violet asked. "I guess I thought…"

"We know what you thought." Al's words were sharp and almost predictable as she prepared for the bias that usually followed.

"We get that a lot." Britt elbowed Al, hoping to soften the team leader's suddenly stern demeanor.

"Yes, we get it so much it's kinda getting old." Al crossed her arms over her chest defensively.

"So, Al is short for Alice," Violet repeated with more interest, and ignored the team leader's posture.

Britt held up a halting hand. "But no one calls her that anymore."

"Why? Alice is such a nice name," Violet said, realizing she hadn't shaken the outstretched hand. "Violet Crest." Her deep dimples appeared with a lopsided smile as she extended a hand out to Al.

"Al is better." The handshake was a quick awkward jerk and the release was abrupt. Britt stepped in before Al could say anything more about her dislike for being called Alice.

"We were about to tie Violet in and assess her ability to climb and repel." PB coiled the belay rope end on the ground, recovering the tether for the next climber.

Al dropped her backpack to the grass and made quick work of stepping into her harness. She kicked out of her sneakers and wriggled her climbing shoes onto her feet. Still kneeling, she looked up at the smaller woman's gear. "Did you double-check her harness, Britt?"

"Sure did, and Greta's, too."

Al clapped her hands together. "Alright, let's do this." She removed a device from her right hip. "Anyone want to tell me what this is?"

Greta's hand flew up. "It's one of these." She twisted her hip. "It's a cam." She squeezed it a few times to pivot the intersecting half-moon mechanism.

"Yes, exactly," Al continued. "When are we going to use these?"

Greta's hand flew up again. "To build a belay?"

"Great answer," Britt said, and she continued to explain proper placement of cams and when to use each size. The exercise was intense and Al admired the seriousness at which PB and Britt delivered the vital information. This was her team and she had complete trust in their abilities even if they sometimes cut loose in reckless ways.

Once Al felt confident their clients understood cams and the other anchoring devices, they moved on to the skill of tying knots.

Greta was a natural. Her hands moved easily to tie in on her harness as she created a stunning figure-eight knot with her climbing rope tail less than eight inches.

"Excellent," Al said as she inspected the knot. "Britt, why don't you and PB take her up the wall."

"So soon?" Britt asked.

"She's ready." Al turned her attention toward Violet. "How are you doing here?" Al did her best to calm the irritated feelings rising up as she watched the woman's hands fumbling with the rope.

"I'm not really getting it." Violet's voice was loaded with frustration as her hands moved with a lack of confidence.

Al held the cluster of twisted rope attached to Violet's harness loops. "You're right, you're not getting it at all."

"This tail is way too long isn't it?" Violet flipped the length of rope that was almost as long as her arm. This much extra length was messy and potentially dangerous.

"Let me ask you this. How do you know if your knot is going to hold?" Al towered over Violet as she inspected the malformed loops for the second time. There was obvious tension between the two of them. The teacher and mentor situation had a level of friction Britt and PB hadn't noticed from their team leader in a long time.

"I looped it around twice and pushed it through the center." Violet tugged the tangle and the length of rope fell to her thigh. Her right hand flapped the dangling end in surrender.

"You've just fallen to the ground." Al was serious as she took the rope. "At the very least, you've twisted an ankle, but maybe you dropped my best friend up there and now we have to carry her out." She pointed her finger at Britt.

Violet's cheeks flushed and her growing frustration was obvious and not productive to accomplishing the goal of the exercise. "I can get it." Her movements weren't aggressive but they were assertive as she took the rope, twisted a knot and attempted to loop the end to her harness and tie in for belaying.

Al didn't speak as she attached a carabiner, tugged it once to set the knot and stripped it from Violet's waist. "You're dead… again."

"I think I need to take a break." Violet tossed her rope and the carabiner into the dirt, turned on her heels and walked over to where PB was working with Greta.

"Scoring points again, hot stuff." Britt slapped Al on the back.

"She's not getting the importance of these knots." Al cracked her neck before bending down to pick up the bundle of rope. The length of Al's arms were almost half her height and she felt the stretch in her calves as she folded in half. She spun the climbing clip around her finger like a Wild West gunslinger as she stood to her full six feet. The height and arm span was an advantage for her as a climber and she took the lead guide position for the Extreme Adventure Group very seriously.

"She's fresh out of college. You remember that, don't you? Know-it-all smart-ass that you are." Britt was only a few inches shorter than Al with a few weeks less experience, but she was respected enough to challenge Al's attitude.

"I was never like that," Al asserted but neither of them could hold back the laugh that followed. Al was confident but she had the credentials to be. Being overly serious since childhood gave her an edge. She was born to dangle from a tether. "Fine, but when she ties a rope, I have to trust it won't kill one of us."

What they were doing on this course was life or death, even though the fall was less than three feet most of the time and there were crash pads all around them. There was a time for fun and games, and this evaluation made no room for either.

"Maybe it's the way she was taught?" Britt stood on her toes to throw an arm around Al's neck. "Bad habits are hard to unlearn."

"Well, if between the three of us we can't teach her, there's no way she goes out with our team. Understood?"

"Understood," Britt said. She was curious about Al's continued frustration with the woman. She also saw something special in Violet's enthusiasm toward the adventure part of their trip. "We'll figure it out."

"Let me take Greta with PB and you can work with Violet." Al reached for her friend's hand, dropped the rope and carabiner into Britt's palm, and walked away.

"I guess I rubbed her the wrong way," Violet said as Britt approached where she was sitting away from the rest of the team.

"It's important to know knots," Britt explained as she held the practice rope to Violet.

Violet took the offered equipment. "All I've done for the last few days is play with my gear." She fanned the cams attached to her harness loops. "I know about over-camming and under-camming. I understand when to use this carabiner and that one." She pulled at each example. "I don't know why I have such a hard time with knot tying."

"Maybe you're trying too hard?" Britt suggested.

"Alice is never going to let me…"

Britt interrupted. "Let's stop right there. If you want to take this trip," she lowered her voice, "you should only ever call her Al."

"That wasn't a joke?" Violet looked up curiously.

Britt chuckled. "Al doesn't have much of a sense of humor out there." She pointed to the forest behind her. "And she definitely has zero sense of humor if you call her by her given name."

"I'll have to work on that," Violet said.

Britt wasn't sure how to read the petite woman as she sat beside her and began the long task of tying in to belay. Violet was strong-willed in a way that would absolutely tug at the rigid lines Al drew around her life to protect her from women like Violet.

Britt hoped the smaller woman made the cut because she was sure the fourteen-day trip would be quite the experience with these colliding personalities.

Chapter Four

A week later, the team sat in a quiet corner in their favorite pub, stealing fries from one another as they sorted through the meticulous notes they'd made about their clients. They had completed extensive evaluations, planning out the next few months of expeditions.

Their new company didn't have an office, or a brick and mortar home, because not one of them stayed in any location long enough to rent one. EAG did most of their business by mobile phone, word of mouth and hand radio.

"Greta Finch?" Al held the client profile and evaluation page, flipping it over to refresh her memory on the high-ropes course and mental toughness tests. This was the time for brutal honesty. Upfront evaluations were more about the success of a trip and the safety of every member on the team.

"Greta, yeah, she was fine," PB said. "I'll work with her on fire-building skills. She's got a lot to learn but she likes to fish. She said she wants to try out her new entomology skills."

"I'll let you go digging for bugs with Greta." Britt chuckled.

"I figured as much," PB teased, snatching the fry from Britt's plate and dunking it in grape jelly before stuffing it in her mouth.

"Gross." Britt pinched her nose.

"You don't know what you're missing."

Britt picked up the single-serve packet and started to read the ingredients. "What even is gelatin?"

"It's what makes it wiggle." PB squeezed Britt's fingers, causing a bubble of jelly to ooze from the packet. "You should come hang out with my family. We'll school you in the art of all things jelly, jam and sweet preserves." The grin that followed was toothy and juvenile and most authentically PB.

Britt held up a hand as she dropped the jelly on a plate. "I'm good."

PB dunked another fry. "Yeah, maybe, but not as good as this." She waved the dripping food before popping it into her mouth.

"Are we done yet?" Al, amused but also not, rested her hands on the paperwork in front of her.

"I'm good," PB said through a mouthful of grape-covered fry.

"Totally good," Britt said, making a gagging sound as she watched her friend chew.

"Excellent." Al made a circle on her paper. "PB, you and Greta can be in charge of food prep on odd days." Al tucked the note to her clipboard. "There's great trout fishing on this route and I can't wait for you to show us what you've got."

"Your bellies will bust, guaranteed," PB said, patting her stomach.

"Sounds perfect." Al shifted to the next page. "Let's move on to Peter Green; what are your thoughts on him?"

"I like Peter, but I think we'd lose him on the first day," Britt shared. She'd worked with the man who was recovering from a freak projectile impalement that kept him away from the first evaluation day.

"Can you believe he was shot with an arrow at a summer camp open house?" PB asked.

Britt stifled her laugh. "By a nine year old."

"It's so ridiculous," PB said.

"I think it would benefit our team to spend more time off trail with him." Al smiled. "With an intense focus on safety protocols."

PB and Britt's laughter interrupted the group sitting behind them in the bar. "How does a nine year old get in front of a grown man and shoot him?" Britt asked, a statement as much as a question.

"Stupidity?" PB answered.

"Carelessness." Al's response lacked humor.

"There had to be rules, right?" Britt was serious for a moment.

PB scraped a fry around the edge of the jelly container. "He broke a few, I guess."

"That's why we have safety protocols." Al made a second check mark beside Peter's name. "And that's why Peter is a no-go for this trip."

"Agreed," PB and Britt said in unison.

"Okay, moving on." Al shuffled the papers. "Next up, we have June Claymor."

"I like her," PB said. "She's improved so much since the last evaluation."

"Britt?" Al looked at her friend.

"I'll take her. PB's right." She nodded. "We can do campsite tear downs and even day meal prep. She's not afraid to try new things which means we can do some wilderness skill building sessions too."

"Sounds good," Al scribbled notes again before moving the page aside and attaching it to her clipboard.

"She said she would even try to clean fish." PB chuckled.

"That would be nice for a change," Al smirked. "I never mind doing it, but it would be nice if one of you two would help out."

"I waste too much when I try to fillet them." Britt said, mostly because she hated the slimy feeling on her hands.

"Uh huh," Al smirked but her expression changed when she realized who was left on their list. "Let's discuss Violet Crest for a minute."

"I really like her." Britt said.

PB, with her mouth full, gave a thumb's up in agreement.

"She struggles with basic skills," Al said, her dislike of the woman made clear by the notations on the evaluation sheet.

"But she's hilarious," PB added.

"Kinda cute, too." Britt looked at Al, waiting for a reaction before winking at PB.

Al circled a few words on the page. "She's not serious enough for what we're about to do."

Britt leaned close to their fearless team leader to read the notes. "Did you just pencil in and circle the word stubborn?"

PB covered her mouth but was unsuccessful at hiding her laughter. "If I didn't know you best, I'd think you had a little too much interest in a certain person named after a flower."

"Knock it off." Al flipped the page over.

Britt snatched the piece of paper. "She scored well on more skill tests than Greta. You're being way too hard on her."

"She can't tie a knot to save her life, or mine," Al insisted.

"You are most definitely having some feelings, boss." Britt was serious as she started to add the numbers along the task evaluation columns. "She scored eight points higher than Greta."

"Knots are everything." Al didn't want to concede.

"Well, Al, we are making a team decision." Britt looked to PB for support.

"Yep," PB agreed, "and the team says you'll have two weeks to help her perfect her skills on the trail because Violet is all yours." Britt wrote Al's name in bold letters beside Violet's.

"I'm doing this in protest." Al added the page to her clipboard.

"We hear you but we also think you're wrong this time." Britt tapped Violet's evaluation sheet. "Wait and see. She'll be an asset."

Al took a slow sip from her drink, trying to justify a reason to fight the decision but incapable of finding one that didn't reveal her initial curious attraction to a woman who was too free spirited for her.

"So we have a team." PB cleared the table.

"We have a team," Al agreed as she took a fry from the plate. "Next order of business: where are we going to take them?" She threw a map in front of them.

"Montana," Britt yelled, slapping the folded paper.

"No, not Montana again," PB said, pushing her hands over Britt's to take the map. "We did Montana three trips ago. How about Colorado?"

"We are not doing Colorado again, either. You just want to hook up with that chick from Rocky Mountain National Park," Britt mocked.

"Jealous?"

"Hell yes, I am," Britt said. "No matter where we are, you manage to get yourself a warm body to—"

"Can you stop objectifying unsuspecting strangers and remember what we are doing here?" Al freed the map from PB and opened it to reveal the country's states. "I'll let the universe decide for us." She picked up her pencil, dropped it on the page and gave it a twirl. It rotated like the spinner on a child's board game, landing on the heavy green shading of a national forest.

"No way. We have to do that spin again," Britt said

PB snatched the pencil. "Stop it! I love the trails there."

"That volcano could erupt." Britt tried listing all the hazards she was aware of in that particular location.

"The fishing is amazing and the park is gorgeous," PB said. "We can do the lookout at Devil's Peak." She liked the area, and started pushing hard for the location.

"It's done. The pencil has spoken." Al removed a fresh trip-route page from her clipboard. "There are a few challenges to this park, and we can try and hit the lookout point at the peak." She reached into her backpack for a national park guide book. She thumbed through until she found the trail map she was looking for. "We could do that hike on day one." She pointed with the tip of her pencil. "It'll be a great way to evaluate if the group can manage some tougher terrain." She pressed her hand into the crease of the page so PB and Britt could see.

Britt folded the tabletop map, intentionally taking her time as she stretched her feet out under the table. "Oh but the critters in that area are not my favorite."

"We've managed before. We know the threats." PB leaned closer. "What's the real reason?"

"I don't know." Britt's tone suggested she did know and was about to tell them. "Maybe it's the snakes." Britt counted on her fingers one by one. "Or maybe the big-ass spiders?" She bent another finger back emphasizing the next. "Maybe it's the bears or it could be the tons-of-fun tick invasion?"

PB waved her off. "Come on."

"Every one of those is a possibility on almost every trip we do." Al began making a list of equipment to help deter all of the hazards Britt had listed. She laid her pencil on the table and looked up at her friend. "If you're not all in for this park you need to be honest and tell us what's the real reason."

Britt was silent for longer than either Al or PB expected.

PB moved closer. "What gives?"

"That park is where all those kids died," Britt whispered. "It's like a cemetery, you know. I don't—"

"People die in every park, in every country, all of the time," PB said, "and anyway, their team leader never should have pushed so hard."

"I'm just not a fan."

"Hey." Al leaned closer, the tone of her voice changing from leader to sister-friend.

"What?" Britt looked up at her.

"We aren't planning to summit," Al said as she slid the paper to Britt. "We'll do some bouldering, easy low-level hikes, survival style camping and fishing."

"You make it sound like summer vacation." Britt chuckled. "I love when you do that."

PB slapped her shoulder. "It'll be easier than any camp you ever attended, plus the group will be small."

"Six packs, three tents. Lighter loads and we can stash supplies ahead of time where we need them." Al tapped the top of her neatly written supply list.

As she studied the paper, Britt dropped her head on Al's shoulder. "You drew a little heart beside bear spray and a skull and crossbones on the bug repellant." Britt slid the page closer to PB.

"That's fucking adorable," PB said.

"So is your bestie over there." Al pointed her pencil toward Britt. "Are you going to be on board with this?" she asked.

"Yes." Britt forced a smile. "I trust you two and I suppose if we have a small group we can manage whatever comes."

"Are you sure you're one hundred percent behind this decision?" Al asked again. "I need all your skills, Britt."

"You'll have all of them. I'm in."

"Yeah, bitches!" PB ate the last of the fries as she started to stack their plates.

"Excellent," Al said. "Let's hit the library and put together the invitation letters for our team."

~~~~~~~~~~~~

"We'll take a clockwise approach on the Timber ridgeway line." Al had a photocopy of the topographical park map laid out on the table in the library's study room. Her notes were spread in a neat line for the team to see. This was typical for them as they mostly worked out of Al's new Outback, Bess. They could count on most communities to have a library with some designated space for small-group activities. It was also the perfect location to access infinite and free resources.

"Clockwise is typical for this trail," PB said. "You sure you don't want to mix it up and go counter-clockwise instead?"

"It's more than forty miles and gets rough here," Al circled the point on the map, "this hill here, the cliff walk here and a few
~~~~~~~~~~~~

places along the river here." She made small red Xs in multiple spots on the trail route. "Let's go with this as the plan." She tapped her pencil against the map. "Considering the skills, and lack of, let's play it safe."

PB helped fold their maps and shuffle the pages into Al's folder. "You think this group can handle forty miles, survival style?"she asked seriously.

Britt took June's background file to study later. "I say we lose two on the way."

PB's eyes widened. "Like lose them, lose them?"

"Nah, not like that." After their hours in the library, Britt was feeling more confident about the location. "I think the hiker least likely to toughen through it is Greta, followed by our little flower."

"So you're guiding the only finisher?" Al laughed as she slid papers in front of each of them. "You know it's gonna muddle everything up if you keep talking like that."

Britt folded her section of the supply list and tucked it into her breast pocket. "I don't believe in tempting fate, but I do believe in my ability to read the terrain."

Al slapped her on the back as she pushed in her chair. "The universe listens." she said, looping her arm over Britt's shoulder.

"Yeah, it sure as hell does."

"So let's take it easy on premonitions and follow the plan that all of us will finish." Al flipped off the lights, leaving the unknowns behind them in the dark. "I'll also plan extraction with Walt and his guys."

"Walt?" P.B. laughed as she pushed through the exit door of the library.

"Your boyfriend, Walter." Britt made kissy lips.

Al shook her head. "He's so not my boyfriend for so many reasons but he is absolutely reliable."

"That's right. Reliable boyfriend Walt." Britt and PB shared a high five as they waited for Al to unlock the car.

"Laugh it up, comedians." Al sat in the driver's seat and tossed her backpack behind her.

Britt pulled on the door handle. "Hey, come on."

"You done?" Al leaned to look at them through the locked passenger doors, waving her fingertips.

"Not even started yet." PB lifted the handle over and over, hoping the action would irritate Al.

Al put her seat back, reclined it and threw her arms behind her head. "That's cool, I've got all day."

"Al!" Britt glared at PB. "You idiot. Stop hurting Bess."

Al leaned closer to the window. "Did you call me an idiot?"

"No," Britt said. "I called her an idiot. Just let us in."

The buttons on the doors popped up. "Get in, you comedians, and let's get the heck out of here."

"Bitch," Britt joked.

Al poked her chest. "I'm the bitch? You just joked about me and Walt."

"He was in love with you," Britt said, and PB nodded silently from the backseat.

"I'm a lesbian." Al put the key in the ignition. "And he's gay." She started the car.

"I'm pretty sure his love for you makes him bisexual."

"Maybe so." Al put the car in reverse, looking over her shoulder and catching PB's snicker. "But I'm always going to be a lesbian."

Chapter Five

"Are you excited?" Greta asked as she jumped from one bus seat to the next for a better view of the drive. She and Violet were the last riders on a mini bus delivering hikers to multiple starting points throughout the area.

"Absolutely excited and a little nervous, too," Violet confessed.

Greta nodded. "I think it's kinda smart to be nervous. There are so many new things happening in the next couple of weeks."

"Wow." Violet pressed her hands against the bus window. "It's absolutely gorgeous so far," she said as the bus crept along a narrow road. She leaned sideways, catching her camera bag on the seat.

"Are you a photographer?" Greta asked.

Violet grabbed the bag belted to her waist. "Yes, I just finished art school."

"And you're spoiling yourself with a survival excursion to celebrate?" Greta's question, delivered with a smirk, was obviously sarcastic.

Violet chuckled. "Something like that. I love being outside and if I want to work anywhere I need to build a portfolio."

"That's so cool." Greta rested her head against the seatback.

Violet shrugged. " Yeah, it's part of the reason why I'm doing this trip."

Greta turned to look at Violet. "Part of the reason?"

"Well, I'm not super adventurous, according to my aunt, so this trip is supposed to break me out of what makes me comfortable."

"Uncomfortable can be exciting." Greta grinned. "Well, sometimes."

"Fingers crossed." Violet held up her crossed fingers.

"Definitely." Greta crossed her fingers in solidarity. "Either way, I hope we have a great time."

"Me too." Violet took out the small film camera, turned it around and waved Greta in for a picture of the two of them. "First shot of the trip."

"That's fun. I hope it turns out." Greta made herself comfortable beside Violet.

"What are you escaping from?" Violet tucked the camera back into the case on her hip.

"Bank teller boredom."

"Oh." Violet was terrible at hiding her agreement at how boring it sounded.

"Yeah." Greta slid sideways as the bus turned from the forest road onto a graded and washboard-rippled gravel driveway. A log-styled wilderness lodge came into view, and the closer they got the more the enormity of the timbers was obvious. What looked like children's toys from a distance were large, rough-hewn tree trunks, stained from age.

"Look at the lodge." Violet gasped.

"The lodge was built over one hundred years ago," the driver said. "I don't think you'll get to stay here, though." He turned into the parking space.

"Yep, you're right; luxury accommodations are not part of this trip," Greta joked as she stood to exit the bus.

"The two outer wings stretching east and west are called the Welcome Wings," the driver added.

"Why?" Greta's mouth was wide open in awe as the view of the wooden castle in the middle of nowhere became more spectacular.

"The daughter of the original architect said the wings of the lodge looked like a giant's arms stretched out to hug the trees and animals around it." He smiled.

"It's amazing what kids see," Greta said. She was intrigued to explore the retreat, and after seeing it up close and personal, she was a little disappointed there wasn't a plan to visit the tourist center before heading out into the wild. "I bet the inside is wonderful."

"Maybe we can stop and check it out at the end of the trip," Violet said. "We'll probably want a soft bed and a hot shower."

"I bet we will. I'll do it if you'll do it." Greta looked up at the building as Violet wandered toward the meeting spot to check-in. The driver dropped their bags on two of the rustic tables.

Violet turned toward the retreating bus driver. "We're supposed to lay out our pack lists?"

The driver nodded before boarding his bus.

"You have pretty handwriting," Greta said as she craned her neck to look at Violet's paperwork.

"Thank you." Violet shrugged. "Side effects of private school."

"Trust-fund kid?" Greta picked up a rock and used it to hold her checklist on the table.

"Hardly." Violet chuckled, copying the action as the wind nearly took the list from her hand. "Parents who wanted the inconvenience of their child to disappear." She pointed to herself.

"Oh, sorry."

Violet shrugged. "Not something you need to be sorry for. Neither should I, really. I'm here now and that's all that matters."

"Great attitude." Greta turned to rest against the table.

"Years of therapy." Violet shrugged and an awkward silence followed.

"I wonder where June is," Greta mused before plopping onto a rustic bench. "Her name was listed in my letter."

"My letter had June's name on it too." Violet sat beside her. "She had her chance to get there, right?"

"More of a chance than most." Greta's nervous nibble on her bottom lip was a clear indication she was concerned about June.

"It sucks for her, but I'm glad the driver didn't leave the two of us behind."

"True. I'm really excited for this hike." Greta pulled her foot up to work out a calf ache. Her bright yellow boot laces contrasted with the gray leg gaiters she wore.

"Nice lace color." Violet smiled as she looked down at the condition of her well-worn pair.

"I've been wearing these for a solid month in preparation." Greta smiled back. "I put the yellow in for good luck."

Violet raised her feet, tapping her boots together. "I know they're kind of beat up but these are my favorite pair to wear when I hike with my aunt."

"You hike with your aunt?" Greta tugged at the laces around her ankle, cinching them tighter in anticipation of the first five miles of the day.

"I do everything with her." Violet tipped her water bottle over to check for leaks before tucking it into the side pouch of her backpack.

"That's really great. I hardly know my aunt."

"Gosh, I can't imagine my world without her in it." Violet looked over her shoulder at the sound of footsteps crunching through the gravel. She felt a flutter in her belly—that nervous excitement that hit just before trying something new.

"Hello campers," Al said as she clipped the sternum strap of her backpack over her chest..

She looks less grumpy than the last time I saw her, Violet thought. She watched Al tighten the strap over her breasts for a little longer than was socially acceptable, and she looked up into questioning and then scolding brown eyes. It wasn't great to get caught checking out a woman, especially when that woman was uptight and unreadable, and frustrated Violet in so many ways.

"Good morning, Al," Greta said.

"Good morning, everyone. I see you're ready to go." Al was all business as PB and Britt stepped up behind her and moved to the table where the backpacks and checklists were laid out. "There's been a change to the team, as you've probably already guessed. June had a family emergency, so we're a team of five."

Al had transferred all her notes and trip plans to a pocket-sized notebook for the trail. She folded over the page she was on so she could pencil in the changes she was about to make.

"Since PB was paired with June, she will be in the lead position for the rough trails, and our go-to guide." Al pointed to the backpacks and asked PB, "Did everyone pass the gear check?"

PB read through Greta's printed checklist, and followed with Violet's, scanning that everything required was in their bags. "They're ready to roll out. Your little swirly check marks are adorable, Violet." She had to point out the cuteness.

"Thanks."

"Trekking poles in hand?" Britt asked and smiled as each fastened the straps around their wrists. "Al, I've adjusted leadership gear for the absence of one hiker."

"Perfect," Al said.

"Violet and Greta, you'll be excited to know you'll get more of my dehydrated surprise jam to compensate."

Britt shook her head. "What mysterious berry are we eating for the next two weeks?"

PB rubbed her hands like an excited child. "Oh, no. It's a surprise."

"It better not make me crap my pants this time," Britt said.

Greta looked up, her fear obvious as she blanched. "What?" Her big brown eyes said more than any words could.

She's going to be fun on the trip, PB thought. "It's a joke." She threw an arm over the woman's shoulder. "No one ever craps their pants."

"No one?" Britt winked, tipping her head toward their leader.

"That was not from the jam," Al defended herself.

"You crapped your pants?" Violet pointed to Al's long, half-covered legs. It was another opportunity to enjoy the rich, tanned skin and the flex of her muscled calves.

"I didn't crap anything." Al leaned close to help her hiking clients fit their backpacks on.

"It was her hiking partner on that trip," PB clarified. "What was her name again?"

"Quincy," Britt and Al said in unison.

"Right, Quincy." PB laughed. "She was allergic to whatever it was."

"We called them murder berries for the rest of that trip," Al added.

"Huckleberries," PB interrupted. "They are not murder berries. They are huckleberries, and most people are fine with them. Plus that jam kicked ass."

"Kicked her ass for sure." Britt laughed as she bounced her backpack into position on her shoulders and lower back.

"That's why both of you received a very extensive allergen questionnaire," Al said. "If everyone's ready, let's get on the trail."

The team set out in a perfectly spaced line. PB was in the lead position, followed by Greta, then Britt. Violet did her best to maintain a consistent pace with the rest of the team but she was also interested in singling out their leader to try and chip away at her annoying barriers.

They were less than a half mile from the lodge when Violet couldn't stand the silence a minute more. "How long have you been guiding hiking trips?" Violet asked.

Al was two full strides behind, having to reduce her pace twice to keep a conservative following distance. "I think it's been ten years, at least."

Violet stopped. "Really?"

Al sidestepped to avoid the smaller woman, grabbing Violet's shoulders to keep her upright. "Yes." She snickered. "I'm pretty sure I was born to live in the wild because no one ever cared to call me in."

Violet laughed. "That's funny."

Al shrugged. "It's easier out here." She waved at the forest around them. "No complications."

"I see," Violet said, and took the subtle tone of disinterest to mean that the conversation was over. Distracted, she tripped over her own feet and Al reached forward, pulling her back on the trail.

"Pay attention." Al's tone was impatient and scolding.

Violet righted her balance, kicked her trekking pole and continued on. She escaped into the stunning forest around them, enjoying the scent wafting from the tall grasses swishing against the wildflowers in the meadow. It was peaceful but also a little too quiet at the far end of their line.

"How's it going back there, team?" PB asked through the hand radio. "I don't have eyes on you, Al."

"We're doing great," Al responded. "Had a little stumble."

"Need first aid?" PB asked.

"All good." Al looked at Violet who'd slowed to walk beside her. "We're back on the trail."

"Roger that," PB said and the team continued.

In a group with three guides and two clients there was less concern about separation, but Al didn't want to put herself into a questionable situation being one-on-one with this woman.

Violet hesitated. "Can I ask you a question?"

"I guess so, because you just did." Al stopped when the petite woman did the same.

Hands on her hips, Violet stared at her group leader. "That's not what I meant."

"Okay." Al snickered. "What did you want to ask?"

Violet felt the barrier between the taller woman and herself but she asked anyway. "Why does everyone call you Al?"

"That's your big curiosity?"

"One of them, yeah."

"It's kinda personal." Al watched Violet stab her trekking pole into the grass as she waited.

"Does that mean you aren't going to answer?"

Al waved her hand to move Violet along. "Yes, it's a question I'm not going to answer."

Violet turned to look at Al. "So personal questions are off the table?"

Al was surprised the woman wasn't pushing for more. "It's the way my world works." She chuckled.

"Okay." It wasn't much of an answer but Violet let it go. "I guess you've been all over the country if you've been doing this for ten years."

"I have." Al stepped closer to the trail edge. "Be careful here." She grabbed Violet's backpack. "There are places along the trail where it drops off." They stopped and Al picked up a stick to toss it over the edge.

"That would be a bit of a fall." Violet took a huge step backward.

"Yeah," Al agreed. "Did you ever see that movie about the bird and the wolf who loved her?"

Violet didn't have to think; she knew the film well. "Yes, that movie is so sad."

"Then you know the part in the movie where the guy says 'walk on the left side'?"

Violet nodded. "I sure do."

"I'd say it is also appropriate in our situation now," Al explained as she pointed at the hidden slope.

"So keep left?" Violet confirmed with a chuckle.

"Right." Al smiled.

Violet stopped walking. "Right?"

"No, left is right."

Violet started to walk. "You are very confusing, Al Hadley."

Al stayed a length behind her, certain she should respond to the continued tension between them. "How am I so confusing?"

"You're always so serious," Violet said.

Al raised her hand to guide Violet away from the ledge. "Seriousness keeps everyone safe."

"I suppose I can respect that."

Al shrugged. "It's just the way I'm built and I think it makes me a better guide and team leader."

Violet stopped, turned around and smiled. "You're doing great so far."

"I appreciate your assessment but we've hardly hiked for half a day." She waved Violet forward. "And at the rate we're going, we'll be an hour behind the team if you don't learn to walk and talk at the same time."

Violet was about to comment on Al's sense of humor when the radio on Al's hip crackled to life.

"We're at rest site one." PB's radio broke the silence and Al was amazed they'd already hiked the first few miles.

"Copy that, we're not far behind."

Violet chuckled. "I guess I'm going to ruin your reputation for timeliness."

Al shook her head. "Believe it or not, you're not the slowest hiker I've ever had on a trip."

Chapter Six

The first stop of the day was a ten minute rest for snacks and water. When Al and Violet caught up with the group, Greta and Britt were already eating handfuls of nuts and berries from a bag.

"You couldn't wait for us?" Al unclipped her backpack and lowered it to the ground.

"What the hell were you doing?" Britt held up her snack bag and Al reached in for a handful. "We've been here five minutes and this is a ten minute stop."

"I had a lot of questions." Violet wasn't shy about telling the truth as she dropped her pack beside PB's.

Al was impressed by the honesty but also put off. She didn't need Violet to speak for her. She was the team leader, capable of making decisions that didn't require explanations or apologies.

"Can't you walk and talk?" PB asked as she came out of the woods with a small shovel and a roll of toilet paper. She pushed them into the outer pouch on her backpack and pulled sweet fern leaves from her pocket.

"We'll work on the challenging skill of walking and talking," Al said as she sat between Britt and Violet. Al's stare lingered on Violet as she picked out the raisins one by one, savoring the sweetness of each with a short moan and delighted smile.

"Why don't you do that so we can stay tight together?" PB rubbed the leaves in her palms, activating the plant oils to clean her hands. "Hit me with some of that."

Britt poured a conservative pile of snacks into PB's hands and passed a bag to Al.

"How's everyone feeling?" Al focused on Greta and Violet.

"I'm feeling so good. I could keep going." Greta grinned.

Al chuckled. "That's good because we've got three miles to our first overnight site and the last mile is all uphill."

"Mostly uphill," Britt corrected. "But the view is stunning and we can stop to take some photos." She tipped her head toward the camera on Violet's hip. "Did you take any pictures?"

Violet shook her head. "Not yet, I was kind of trying not to fall over the ledge."

"Oh my gosh, that was scary," Greta said. "Did Al tell you to keep left like the drivers do in Europe?" Greta smiled as she referenced Britt's warning.

"No, Al made a super cute movie reference," Violet shared.

"The bird movie?" PB shook her head, knowing that Al used a handful of books and movies as a test of personality, good taste and, most importantly, character. "That's not how to measure a good person, you know?"

"What? It's a great movie and you can tell a lot about someone if they've seen it," Al argued.

"Like what?" Britt asked, hoping she would share her quirky test of compatibility.

Al looked at the group of people in front of her. "Never mind." She waved off Britt's question before disappearing into the woods.

"Your boss is frustrating," Violet said. She sipped from her water canteen.

"The tough ones always have a soft heart," Greta whispered.

PB laughed. "You got that from a bird movie?"

"And from the second test day when she talked about climbing." Greta re-tied her loose gaiter.

"Oh yes, the way she went on and on about free climbing," Violet agreed.

Britt tipped her head toward the tree-line Al had escaped through to explain her perspective. "Climbing is like nothing else. There's no better way to understand failure and success than when you've got one hand gripping a wall with two fingers, and everything depends on these little muscles," Britt made hooks with the fingers on her right hand, holding onto an imaginary rock, "and your thighs feel like solid steel when your toes are holding you in a way that defies gravity. I can't think of any experience that feels more like home. " She smiled as she swiped the trail mix residue on her pants.

PB nodded. "Oh yeah, I can't imagine my life without all of this." She waved her arms to include the vastness of their wilderness.

"I second that." Al stepped out of the trees. "I'll never have a nine-to-five."

"Yeah," Britt agreed.

"Absolutely." PB held up a hand to high five and Britt slapped it.

"You've all got it." Greta stood to get her water bottle.

"You've all got it, for sure," Violet said.

"Got it?" Al asked, clearly confused as to what "it" was.

"A passion for the outdoors, for climbing," Greta answered.

Al fished her arms through her backpack and secured it across her chest. "I don't think you can do what we do if it isn't part of you." She unscrewed the rubber cover on her trekking pole, revealing the metal tip.

"It has to be, because sometimes you have to push beyond what you think you can do." Britt followed Al's lead as she removed the rubber tips from her poles and zipped them into the thigh pocket of her pants.

"Take the rubber covers off, everyone." Al held the caps in her palm. "You'll need to dig in a bit as we ascend."

Greta didn't say another word as she sipped her water and tucked the trekking pole caps inside her backpack.

Violet interrupted the silence. "Do you mind if I ask how the three of you met?"

PB looked at Britt, and Britt looked at Al, each asking silent permission to share the personal story.

Al tugged her wrist strap. "We met in therapy."

PB's eyes went wide and Britt fought to hide a grin. Violet could tell it was not the truth as they giggled like children.

"No you did not," Violet accused.

Britt laughed. "Therapy? That's how you're going to tell it, Al?"

Al shrugged. "It was kinda therapeutic."

"But it wasn't therapy," PB interrupted.

Britt shoved Al. "Summer camp isn't therapy."

"It was, for me," Al insisted.

PB smacked her forehead. "We met at a camp for city kids." She adjusted her backpack for the next part of their hike. "I was a bit of a street rat. My ma thought I was getting into too much trouble so she and my grandma sent me to six-week sleep-away camp."

"I think we all had pretty much the same story," Britt said, and Al nodded.

"How old were you?" Greta asked.

"Eight," the three of them said in unison.

"Eight?" Greta asked, unsure that she heard correctly with the overlapping voices.

P.B. checked her boot laces before stepping toward the trail. "Yeah, we were tearing up the playgrounds."

"At eight?" Violet asked, pausing for Greta to pass her so she could take up the spot between Britt and Al.

Al's voice dropped lower. "Mama didn't mess around."

"She sure the hell didn't." Britt chuckled.

"So you met at camp and then what?" Greta asked.

"My mama called Al's mom and the two of them put us in the same local Boys and Girls club where PB was," Britt explained. "That one," she pointed beside her at Al, "she snuck into the boxing gym one day and scurried up the climbing rope. She was hanging there, laughing and giggling, and when we didn't get caught, we kept doing it."

"If you look at the gym ropes now, they're twenty-five feet off the ground," PB said. "She could have been hurt, like seriously hurt or even killed, if she fell."

"Obviously you didn't fall." Violet turned to look at her team leader, who was grinning. Al's smile was big, and Violet thought she looked beautiful with the sunlight reflecting in her eyes.

"I didn't fall but eventually we got caught," Al admitted. "Britt turned eleven and she dared me to do it using only my arms."

Violet stopped and Al walked into her. "Were you that strong at eleven?"

The team circled together for the rest of the story.

"She was scrawny." Britt laughed. "Without all that muscle, she weighed less than two wet socks."

"Shut up," Al said. "I was eleven. Everyone is scrawny at eleven and yes, I made it to the top."

"How did you get caught?" Greta asked.

"PB, you want to tell 'em?" Britt chuckled.

PB stared at Britt with the most passionate non-verbal *no* possible.

Britt held up a hand at Greta, and quickly stared down PB. "Wait, don't be like that."

"It was a misunderstanding," Al said with kindness in her tone.

"She narced on us," Britt blurted out, and PB crossed her arms defensively.

"She told the truth," Al defended.

"Got us busted and we had to have adult supervision."

PB interrupted the storytelling. "We wouldn't be climbing today if I'd lied."

"Maybe," Britt said.

"There's no *maybe* about it. They put up a climbing wall six months later," PB said.

"Okay, yeah."

"So that's our story." Al reached for her friends and pulled them closer to her. "We're here now and we've been best friends for over twenty years." She held each around the shoulder and hugged them as close to a strangle as was acceptable in the situation.

"That's right," Britt squeaked. "Best climbing team around."

"Except for my aunt, I don't think I have a single person I've known for more than five years." Violet stepped around the huddle and snapped a picture of the EAG team.

"You're pretty quick with that camera," Al said.

"I'm always looking at the world through a camera, even when I'm not," Violet explained.

"That's kinda neat," Greta said.

"Neat." Violet chuckled as she repeated the word. "Yeah, I guess it is."

"Can I have a copy of that photograph when you get them printed?" PB pointed at the camera.

"Sure." Violet took a less candid shot as PB posed. "You can be my first customers." She grinned. "Free of charge, of course."

"You won't make a living that way." Al stepped out of the hug.

"Probably not, but I might make friends." Violet tucked the camera back in the case on her hip.

"Maybe." Al waved the hikers forward. "I guess we'll have to see how your photographs turn out."

Chapter Seven

"How's everyone in the back?" PB radioed an hour after they'd left their second snack break.

"How are you doing?" Al asked Violet, who was clearly more excited about the scenery than the actual hike they needed to finish.

"I'm doing great." Violet had stopped again to photograph the odd-colored mushroom draped in bird feathers on the forest floor. The straps of her backpack and front of her shirt were smeared with dirt and debris from laying on her belly but she was excited to see what developed from the angle she'd achieved.

"We're good." Al shook her head. She spoke into the radio clipped onto her backpack's chest loop. "Not sure how far behind you we are."

"We just hit overnight site one." PB's voice crackled through the radio.

"Copy that." Al poked her trekking pole into the rock and it stuck like a dagger. "My guess," she raised her voice so Violet could hear, "is we're about a half mile from your location."

Violet seemed completely disinterested until she noticed Al's straight-line lips and furrowed brow. "Am I slowing us down again?" she asked, and the subtle raise at the end of her question caused Al to raise her right eyebrow.

Al's crossed arms were almost enough of an answer. "Slowing, no. We've stopped, Violet." The team leader's tone was clipped, pointing out the obvious answer.

"So that's a yes."

Al shook her head with a snicker. "Yes, and the team is going to need some of the gear in my backpack and in yours."

Violet took one final photograph and tucked the camera into its pouch. "I'll stop taking pictures."

"That would be helpful," Al said. She was struggling with the woman's inability to stay on the trail. Violet's need to capture her surroundings wasn't selfish as much as it was distracting from the experience of nature. Al felt she was missing out on the intention of EAG's excursion. Violet was kind and curious, but she also challenged her team leader and the rigid style of personality Al wore as protection.

"Do we need to run?" Violet's grin was playful as she swiped dirt from her chest.

Al shook her head. "We don't need to run but we do need to move." She sounded frustrated as she yanked the freestanding pole.

"Sorry." Violet turned sharply and made her way up the trail.

"You don't need to be sorry. You need to remember that we're a team here and we need to work better at staying together."

"I'll try to remember," Violet said just above a whisper as she slowed to walk beside Al.

"That'll make this easier." Al wiped her face, not because she was hot or sweaty but because she didn't want Violet to see her smile. They walked side by side in silence and as the slope of the ground increased, Violet's breathing labored.

Al's body didn't seem to react to the change at all. "Are you some kind of super human?" Violet huffed.

Al chuckled. "I am not."

"Why doesn't this incline affect you?" Violet's foot slipped on a loose patch of stone as she huffed.

Al released a trekking pole, freeing her left arm to catch Violet as she stumbled.

"See." Violet inhaled slowly. "Super human."

"Nah." Al waited for Violet to catch her breath before helping her to the grass. "I'm experienced. That's all."

"Thanks." Violet steadied herself and continued to the top of the hill. "Wow," she gasped as the lake came into view. "Is that even real?"

Al snickered. "It's real. Stunning, isn't it?"

"The water's so blue." Violet reached for the camera on her hip.

Al's hand covered Violet's. "Can we get down there first?" She pointed at the campsite where the rest of the team stood waving at them.

"Oh, right," Violet whispered. "I'm supposed to stop until we meet up with the team."

Al didn't respond as she tipped her pole toward the trail and led her client to the open space where the rest of the group waited.

Site one was little more than a patch of dirt, with a giant log crossing through to divide the space in half. The view was more than spectacular as the forest tree line rolled out toward the greenest pasture of tall grass. Not far beyond was the most picturesque shimmering blue lake Violet had ever seen in real life.

"So glad you could make it," Britt joked. "You need to keep that thing strapped in while we're hiking." She pointed at Violet's dirt-stained shirt and then more directly flicked her finger against the camera bag on her hip.

"Yes, I'll try to behave." Violet dropped her backpack beside the others and noticed a small ring of rocks with sticks and branches inside. "Message received."

PB and Greta collected gear from Al as they set out to try their hand at trout fishing for the team's lunch. "We'll need a cooking fire." PB pointed at the rock ring she'd started to build. She tucked the fly rods under her arm and smiled when Greta began asking questions as they disappeared into the forest.

"We're on kitchen duty." Al unclipped the side pouch from her backpack.

"Yep, I kind of figured." Violet was disappointed she'd have to wait to photograph the lake. For the first time, she reminded herself this was a team trip and there was no "I" in team.

As Britt rummaged through her backpack, she felt the tension between her friend and their client. "I think I'll go out and get more firewood and collect some water." Britt removed a collapsible bladder from Al's backpack. She squeezed the button on her radio for a check and everyone jumped.

"Radio's good." Al held a thumbs-up.

"I'll be back." Britt disappeared into the woods on her way to take a lot of time filling the water bladder and avoiding the mood that had arrived at camp.

Al and Violet were alone again and worked together in silence. Al used the giant log that separated the site as a work top, anticipating they'd have fish to cook.

Violet wandered, picking up sticks and dry plant matter to start a fire. The silence was daunting, and Violet wondered if the whole week was going to continue like this.

"I can prep food here," Al whispered to herself as she brushed the spot where the bark was missing. They were not the first hikers to use this downed tree as a work surface.

Violet seized the opportunity to end the silence. "I should start the fire now, right?"

"I think so. We'll need a patch of coals for the fish."

Violet chuckled. "Are you sure they'll catch some?"

"PB is pretty good in the river and the way Greta talks about it, she's some kind of fish whisperer."

"She talks to fish?" Violet was skeptical.

Al chuckled. "According to her, yes."

"I'll look forward to silent fish for lunch." Violet adjusted the rocks around the burn pit to allow for air circulation, and took her time settling a pile of tinder on the flattest stone. The collection of sticks she planned to use as kindling lay close to her knee.

Al watched from the opposite side of the campsite, appreciating Violet's approach to fire-making. It wasn't a skill every client had. Violet could have used a lighter or a book of matches but instead pulled a magnesium bar and striker from her backpack's inner pocket. This camper had built a fire or two in her lifetime.

Al was even more intrigued as Violet whittled a healthy pile of filings from the magnesium bar, flipped it over and struck the back of her knife against the flint. Al got a real view of the knife's blade when Violet laid it down to adjust the nest of tinder. This was not a sporting-good store fixed blade knife. The unique combination of leather, brass and hardwood handle material came from a talented bladesmith. It was obviously special, much like the one Al had buried in her pocket.

"Come on you stinky sticks, light," Violet whispered under her breath. She wanted to impress Al. Even with her back turned, Violet could sense Al's curious gaze. The next sparks hit the magnesium shavings, creating smolder that turned into flame. On her knees in the dirt, Violet bent closer to blow on the nest of tinder. "Yeah, baby, I still got it." She pursed her lips as she whispered a controlled breath into the fire she held in her hands. "Blessed be."

The tiny smolder puffed into flames as Violet fed the sticks in one by one until she was tending a raging fire. Al had to admit fire-making was definitely a skill Violet brought to the team.

"Impressive," Al said, her hands buried deep in her pockets.

"Thanks," Violet said with a smile, finally feeling a chip break from the barrier between them.

"We have waterproof matches, you know." Al wanted to smack herself for the comment as soon as it flew from her mouth. There was no reason to continue to create distance between herself and this woman.

Barrier chip back in place, Violet shook her head. "Matches are too easy." She made a tripod with three sections of fallen tree limbs. "Plus, I like to test myself."

Al relaxed her forearms on top of the log, casual while maintaining the space between them. "Who taught you how to make fire with a magnesium striker?"

"My aunt."

"Your aunt makes a lot of fires outside?"

Violet laughed. "She makes fires under a full moon." She pointed skyward, twirling her knife in the air like a wand. "She dances by firelight to celebrate Solstice, Samhain, every other wheel of the year festival, and a few I've never celebrated. And I'm pretty sure she does all of it so she can make fire the way I just did."

"What's Samhain?" Al relaxed her chest against the log.

"Halloween to most of the world, but to my aunt, it's a sacred night when the veil between the living and the dead is very thin."

"Are you're saying she's a w—"

Violet interrupted. "A solitary practitioner of the old ways."

"Oh."

"Yep, and she practically raised me to be a free spirit." Violet tucked her knife into the sheath on her right hip.

"So I can blame her for our late arrivals at camp."

Violet looked up, expecting that straight-line smirk, but was delighted to see an actual grin. It was sarcastic, but still felt like a win. "Maybe, but I'd never mess with her. She's feisty."

"You must be like her?"

Violet smiled. The idea that she was like the woman she most admired made her happy. "I guess I kind of am." She continued to fuel her fire.

"I'm noticing you're left handed." It was more an observation than a question, and Al hadn't meant to vocalize it.

Violet looked at her hand as she secured the strap over the knife's guard. "I'm both, really. Another thing my aunt encouraged."

"They say ambidextrous people are super creative."

"They do, do they?" Violet teased.

"So you're not just a photographer, you're an artist, too?" Al asked, but before she could hear the answer, Britt's voice came over the radio.

"Hey, boss."

"Yep, go," Al answered.

"PB's headed back to camp. When she gets there, can you come down and give us a hand?"

Al looked up, locking eyes with Violet as she responded, "I'll be right there."

PB met Al at the edge of camp. "Greta and Britt have a tangled mess but there are a few trout in the basket." She set down the filled water bladder. "There's also a little pile of firewood."

Al grabbed the fillet knife from the rucksack. "I'm on it. I'll be back. Keep that fire going." She pointed with the sheathed knife, tucked the blade into her pocket and disappeared into the thick of trees.

"Nice fire," PB said as she sat beside Violet.

"Thanks."

PB used her knife and a smaller branch to begin splitting the log she'd balanced on her shoulder while carrying the water. She didn't look up as she hammered down on her blade. "I'm sure Al has mentioned it, but we should work harder to stay together as a group."

Violet blew the flames one more time before sitting back on the heels of her boots. "Yes, she mentioned it quite a lot."

"It's a safety thing."

Violet nodded. "I understand that. I didn't realize it would be so beautiful out here."

"City girl?" PB passed two pieces of firewood to Violet.

"I'm an all-over-the-place girl, honestly."

"There are forests all over the place, aren't there?"

Violet laughed. "Obviously, but I guess I wasn't looking as closely as I have been today."

"That's the magic of the outdoors," PB smiled, but it was clear she wasn't joking. "It casts a spell that's impossible to break."

"Is your entire Extreme Adventure Group under the same spell?" Suddenly chilled, Violet rubbed her hands near the flames.

"Do you believe in such things?" PB sat on the ground beside Violet.

"When I was a girl, my parents sent me away." Violet poked the fire with the longest stick in the pile. "I ended up with my aunt."

"Sent you away? That's horrible," PB said.

Violet stared at the flames. "Looking back at it now, it turns out it was a gift."

"Lemons into lemonade?" PB snickered.

Violet shrugged. "Something like that. My aunt is so sweet and humble but most of all she believes in what most people can't see."

"What does that mean?"

"I could tell you but—"

"A hand here." Al walked into camp, one arm loaded with firewood and the other balancing a slice of wood with a pile of fish filets.

Violet was on her feet as fast as PB. "That's an impressive catch of fish."

"I hope you're hungry," Al said as she passed the logs and set the filets on top of the makeshift workspace.

"Where are Britt and Greta?"

Al shook her head. "They're still working on the line for the second pole. Apparently Greta has advanced skills in tangling lines, not so much in actually getting the line into the water to hook fish."

"That bad?" PB asked.

"Worse." Al laughed. "She said she'd make it up to us by cooking the fish."

"Can she cook?" Violet asked.

"Yes, she can cook," Greta said as she laid the bundle of fishing line on the ground beside her backpack. "It's getting too dark to see but I got most of it."

Violet studied the palm-sized pile of line tangled with sticks, green plant pieces and something brown.

"We've got enough for dinner, and breakfast is something PB likes to surprise us with on the first morning," Al explained as she crossed her long legs in front of the fire.

"You'll love it. I promise." PB rubbed her hands together like a mad scientist. "I'm going to forage for some greens; anyone want to learn?"

Greta shook her head. "I'm cooking."

"I'll go." Violet raised her hand like a schoolgirl.

"No camera," PB said.

Violet nodded and unbuckled her belt to remove the camera bag.

"Okay, you can come."

"Britt and I will strike camp." Al opened the top of her backpack. "Three and two for tent setup." She pointed to the people in the team, grouping Greta, PB and Brit, while counting herself paired with Violet.

PB powered up and keyed her radio to check it. "All good."

"Get out of here before it gets too dark."

~~~~~~~~~~~

"That was absolutely amazing." Al scraped her plate into the fire. "There's not much that's better than fresh river trout."

"It was very good," Violet agreed as she collected the dishes from the rest of the team. She turned toward Al. "I'm going to run these down to the lake and wash them. Would you like me to bring more water to boil?"

"All of the canteens are full and ready to go for the morning. We can boil one more pot to cool overnight." Al picked up the empty water bladder. "I'll help you with this."

The walk to the river's edge was quick but quiet as each woman struggled with finding a topic of conversation. Violet didn't understand why Al made small talk seem complicated.

"You didn't have to come with me." Violet squatted near the water's edge. She was wondering why Al had come with her if she was going to continue the silent treatment. "You're probably
~~~~~~~~~~~

sick of my weirdness already." She swished the plates in the water.

"You aren't weird, Violet." Al stepped out of her pants, revealing her long muscled legs and a pair of skin-hugging shorts. "You're focused on the newness of the wilderness and that can be very distracting."

"Is that a kind way of calling me weird?"

"It isn't anything other than what I said." Al walked into the deeper water, floating the bladder until it was full.

"You mean that, don't you?" Violet asked as she stacked the plates in a pile. She watched her team leader walk from the lake, the light of the moon bright enough to illuminate the ripple of waves caused by the breeze on the water.

"If I say it, I mean it." Al laid the bladder on the shore beside the pile of plates. "I'm not a complicated person."

"If you were sitting where I am right now, you might find that hard to believe."

Al stepped closer to Violet, picked the smaller woman up and moved her three feet away. She stood in the position that Violet had held seconds before, essentially switching places. "No, I believe it here, too."

Violet turned to look at the smirking woman. "Wow, did you really just do that?"

"Sure did." Al sat on the rocks.

"Like I said, you're more complicated than any woman I've ever known."

"So you're saying you haven't known a lot of women?" Al was being incredibly sarcastic, and she knew it, but there was some kind of spell at work in this forest between Violet and herself, and she needed to break it. Al took off her zip-up jacket and untucked her shirt from her shorts. She wore only a sports bra underneath. "The water's warm. You should come in."

"I'll wait here and watch for creepy crawlies."

Al waded out to her hips. "You're volunteering to be my protector?" She chuckled.

Violet shook her head. "I'll mostly scream for the rest of the team and call them on this." She plucked the device from the pile of clothes.

"Make sure you turn it on." Al pointed at the radio in Violet's hand before falling backward into the water.

Violet rotated the dial and it squelched at the same time Al disappeared with a splash. Violet clicked her flashlight, scanning the top of the lake for Al to reappear. Moments later, Al was walking toward shore fifteen feet from where she'd gone under.

"Feel better?" Violet asked.

"I feel absolutely amazing." Al collected her clothes and the water bladder. "Are you ready to go back?"

Violet shook her head. "Can I sit here a little longer?" She hugged her knees to her chest.

"Sure, if you'd like." Al set the water down so she could pull her shirt on.

Violet's head turned, resting on her knees as she watched Al cover her body. "You're going to be all wet."

Al chuckled. "It's water. I can handle it."

"I suppose you can."

They sat together for a few minutes until Violet couldn't contain her observations. "It's almost as beautiful out here in the dark as it is during the day."

Al looked up at the sky full of stars. "I can't imagine trading in this night sky for anything."

Violet didn't respond. She sat in the silence that followed, agreeing without words that the absence of the outside world created the peace that she craved.

Chapter Eight

"We should head back." Al slid her boots on over her bare feet and tucked her socks into the pocket of her pants.

Violet picked at the rocks along the shore. She was finally enjoying the way she and Al could sit in silence. She knew the rest of the team must be finished with setup and there was no way they'd go to sleep without checking in. "Will they be worried we've been gone so long?"

"Not at all." Al waved the radio before clipping it on her belt. "I'm pretty efficient and very comfortable in the woods." She stood and offered a hand to help Violet from the ground.

"You do give the impression of self sufficiency." Violet took hold of the offered hand. "Thanks."

"No problem." Al picked up the water bladder and the plates. "Survival of the fittest isn't a joke out here." She waved Violet ahead of her. "You go first."

"Are you sending me ahead as bait for the wild things?" Violet was only half joking.

"Uh." Al pointed at Violet's back pocket. "You've got the flashlight."

"Right." Violet laughed as she clicked the power button and directed the beam along the ground. It was obvious to Violet that there was still tension between them, but there was also something else. Why did Al need this professional wall? She wanted answers even if it was only to make her less weird in front of the team leader and the rest of the group.

"Hey boss, we were about to check on you two." Britt studied Al, noticing her damp hair and the shirt clinging to her chest. "Did you push her in?" She poked at the smaller woman.

"No," Violet said. "I would never do that."

Britt could see her joke missed the mark. "Sorry, I was being funny and Al was behaving predictably. She has a hard time resisting mountain lakes."

"Britt isn't wrong," Al admitted, waving up and down her wet body, "obviously." She tucked the dinner plates inside a backpack and took a few seconds to survey their site. "Camp set up looks good."

"Greta was a great help." PB poked the embers in the dying fire. "She could hardly keep her eyes open so we sent her off to sleep."

"It was a physical end to a very physical day." Al looked to Violet. "You should turn in, too."

Violet watched as Al removed clothing from her backpack before clipping her bag to the long rope and pulling it up into the tree. "I was about to ask which one is mine," she said.

"You're with Al," PB hitched a thumb behind her, "in the blue one. Bed rolls are all laid out."

"Thanks." Violet stepped behind the women and unzipped the tent door. "Goodnight, everyone," she said before removing her shoes and climbing inside. She needed to think about the last hour in the moonlight, and her curious attraction to this woman who mostly frustrated and intimidated her. The dive into the lake was a glimpse of a person she wanted to know more about. It was only their first day—she'd have time to settle this curiosity and work on whatever she was feeling.

"You staying up, boss?" Britt asked as she poured water from the bladder into the pot.

"Are you planning to boil the drinking water before you put out the fire?" Al pulled her shirt over her head.

"That's what we talked about," PB answered.

Al stepped out of her pants and carried them toward the tent. "The sky's pretty clear. Maybe enjoy some stargazing tonight and I'll take care of the water tomorrow night with Violet."

"Sounds good," Britt said. "Sleep well."

"I'll do my best," Al said. She unzipped the tent, a typical two-person space ultimately designed for the comfort of one. Violet was on her back, her eyes open as she rested atop the sleeping bag.

"Are your boots dry?" Al loosened her laces to dry her own.

"They aren't too bad," Violet whispered. "They'll be good in the morning."

Al turned her back to Violet and removed her wet clothes. Violet's eyes widened as she watched the muscles of Al's back and shoulders flex in the dim light. She wasn't expecting the immediate feelings the team leader's partial nudity provoked.

Violet rolled to her side. "You didn't want to stay out and enjoy the fire?" Her voice trembled and she internally criticized her lack of control. It wasn't the first time she'd ever seen the body of a beautiful woman, and it probably wouldn't be the last.

"I think the swim and the starlight were better than the fire." Al tied her shirt and shorts to the strings dangling from the center of the tent. "Plus, I wanted to get out of my wet clothes."

"Do you do that a lot?" Violet asked.

"Take off my clothes?" Al chuckled. "Every night."

"That's not what I meant." Violet rolled onto her back.

"I know what you meant, and yes," Al said. "I love swimming in the cold water."

"You must have warm blood." Violet felt a chill even though the addition of a second body heated the tight space of the tent. "I'd still be struggling to get warm."

"Maybe you shouldn't try it then."

"Maybe." Violet rumpled her sleeping bag so she could climb inside. "I'm not a huge fan of cold weather, either."

"You can move closer to me if you get cold at night." Al laid atop her bedroll. "From what I hear, I put off a lot of heat when I'm sleeping."

Violet's curiosity peaked. "From what you hear?"

"Weird way to put it, I guess. PB and Britt tease me because I'm always in boxers and a tank top when I'm sleeping. They say I'm naked." Al turned toward Violet, waving her hands in front of herself. "But obviously I'm not naked."

"I'll remember to sleep closer if I get cold," Violet said.

Al held up a hand. "I'm not suggesting anything." She planted her foot on the floor of the tent. "I'm locked in right here. You're absolutely safe with me in the tent. I'm not going to budge."

Violet thought about the comment. About what it meant for Al to keep their close proximity chaste. Did the team leader just reveal something personal? "Are you saying you sleep with girls?" Violet stared up at the roof of the tent, afraid to look at the person beside her.

"Women," Al said.

"What?" Violet whispered.

"I sleep with women," Al whispered back.

"Plural?"

Al laughed, followed by a snorty chuckle. "Not at the same time, if that's what you mean."

"That's not what I meant at all."

"I didn't think so," Al said. "Do you?"

The silence lasted a few seconds. "Sleep with women?" Violet asked for clarification.

"Yes." Al made the sound deep in her throat.

"Uh huh."

"Hmm," Al responded but didn't say another word.

Violet rolled to her side, her eyes staring directly into Al's shadowed face. "What does hmm mean?"

"Nothing."

Violet pulled the sleeping bag around her face. "I don't believe you."

"I was about to say the same to you," Al replied.

"You don't believe I sleep with women?" Violet huffed.

"You come off a little…" Al paused, unsure she wanted to say what she was thinking.

"A little what?" Violet felt her face flush.

"Straight."

The gasp was loud. "I do not."

Al rolled to look at the woman who was bundled up so tightly that only her face was showing. "You really do."

"Well, you come off as a burly butchy dyke." Violet knew there was truth in her comment, but this woman who'd shown a vulnerable softness just hours before was revealing a frustrating full-fists-up fighting persona.

"I am a burly butchy dyke." Al chuckled. "What you see is pretty much what you're gonna get."

"Ugh, well I've never dated guys, so there's that. Think whatever, do whatever you want with it." Violet rolled away from the team leader regretting, not for the first time, that she was paired with the frustrating woman.

Al stared at the fluffy blanket-covered backside of the woman beside her. Violet Crest was getting under her skin in a way few people had before. She might be a problem if Al didn't find a way to keep a safe distance between them. She rolled over, locking her bare foot on the tent floor, positioning herself away from the pint-sized powerhouse of a woman.

~~~~~~~~~~

In the darkness, Al felt the smaller woman snuggle in close to her. The night air around them was cold as she tried to move away from the warm body. She kept her left foot planted on the tent floor as promised, but she couldn't do much about the person making herself comfortable in a quest for Al's body heat.

Her eyes were wide open as she listened to the sounds of nature. It was going to be a very long night.

~~~~~~~~~~

Oh, shit, Violet thought as she felt herself snuggled against the body of another person. It took a few breaths for her to realize where she was and who this warm body belonged to. It was not okay to touch anyone without consent and here she was snuggling through her sleeping bag with a practical stranger. There was no way to casually release the hold. Without saying a word, she wriggled away from Al, rolled onto her stomach and did her best to fall back to sleep. "*Control your breathing*," she thought as she squeezed her eyes shut. She could do this, all she had to do was pretend to sleep.

~~~~~~~~~~

Violet didn't know how long she'd slept but the sound of the tent zipper woke her. Hesitant, she turned toward the center to see Al stuffing her bed roll into a compression bag.

"You don't have to get up yet," Al whispered. "I'm just prepping for this morning's tear down and I'm on breakfast duty with PB."

"Oh—kay," Violet grumbled.

"You've got thirty minutes before you have to begin moving around." Al piled her bundles near the tent door and shoved her feet into her boots. The maneuver seemed rushed. "I'll give you privacy." Al scooted out the tent, grabbing her gear and leaving Violet alone with the embarrassing memory of the early morning snuggles.
~~~~~~~~~~

"Thank you," Violet whispered, and before the tent door zipped closed, Al's head popped through.
"You're welcome."

Chapter Nine

"Let's pack it up," Al said, wiping the water from the last of their breakfast plates. It wasn't the meal PB had planned, but after the huge haul of trout the night before, there was enough fish to mix with dried eggs. PB's big breakfast could wait until tomorrow. "If we set a solid pace, we'll be able to strike camp before sunset."

"I hate striking in the dark, especially at the next site," Britt said.

"Why?" Greta asked as she double-knotted her boot laces.

"It's the snakes," PB joked, but no one laughed.

"Gaiters on, everyone," Al said. She looped her laces around and over her calf.

"We'll definitely see snakes in the next few miles," Britt said. "I just know it."

"I'm not a super fan of them," Greta said.

"You're gonna see all kinds but you'll mostly want to look out for the rattlers." PB made a claw with her hand and clamped on to Britt's ankle. "Don't worry. If Britt sees one, you'll hear about it."

Violet laced her gaiter a little tighter. "Are you going to point them out?"

"Oh she will point them out, alright." PB chuckled. "She's gonna scream like crazy."

"Don't say it!" Britt pointed at PB.

"That's why we call her—"

Britt covered PB's mouth and pointed a stern finger at her. "Don't!"

PB gave the palm of Britt's hand a swirly wet lick and it fell away. She ran behind Al, hiding as she said, "That's why we call her Britt the Bitch."

"Ugh, gross." Britt wiped her hand on the butt of her pants. "That's so rude."

"Knock it off you two." Al shrugged PB away, laughing as she added, "Honestly, Britt, you were a little bitch that trip. I mean, it was a garter snake. Harmless on the scale of one to it might kill you."

"It was a snake. You can never be too safe." Britt smacked the gaiter on her leg. "Plus you made me lead and that means I find them first." She stabbed her trekking pole into the dirt. "I'll skewer 'em today."

"I'm not eating rattlesnake," PB hissed.

"Are we gonna eat snakes?" Greta turned sharply toward Al.

Al shook her head. "Not if I can help it. We've got fish on the menu or dehydrated beef as a backup if the lines get tangled again."

"We'll have fish," Britt reassured her. "I'll make sure we have plenty of fish."

Al walked the perimeter of their site, collecting unused kindling and branches, and returning them to the thick of the forest. When she was mostly satisfied, she waved the team forward. "Let's hit it."

"Lead on, my bitch." PB cackled and Al shook her head. "No respect."

Britt turned and the rest of them followed her along that day's more rustic trail.

Al took the time to double-check their site, making sure to return the stump to the forest, and kicking the rocks back toward the shore. "Looks good," she said as she took her position behind Violet.

"Britt screaming about snakes was supposed to be funny, right?" Violet asked, without humor in her tone.

Al wasn't convinced Violet thought it was funny. "Not a fan of snakes?"

Violet slowed so Al could catch up with her. "I like snakes. I'm a fan of most animals, really."

"Are you going to tell me that your *old ways* aunt is also a veterinarian?"

"Funny you should say that because I'm in veterinary school." It was absolutely untrue but Violet wanted to take the swagger out of this profoundly cocky woman's step.

"You are?" Al stopped.

Violet shook her head. "No, I'm not." She flicked the camera bag on her hip. "I'm a photographer, but you believed me for a second, didn't you?"

"I did."

"Hey." PB yelled for their attention. "Greta just asked Britt if we ever come across hot guys on the trail." PB laughed. "Britt told her she is more interested in hot chicks. I said I don't care—hot guy, hot chick; doesn't matter to me—and now she wants to hear your thoughts, Al."

"I can't say that I've ever wondered about any guy being hot or not," Al yelled.

"Violet?" PB put her on the spot.

"Not into guys much either." It felt good to say it out loud with them. Violet stopped, excited to experience comradery in the small group. The EAG team did an excellent job creating a space where she felt safe to be herself.

Al stood close to Violet and nodded toward the women ahead, watching them fade into the distance. "You know, I'm going to get demoted if we keep wandering into camp twenty minutes behind the leader."

Violet stabbed her poles into the dirt. "Can *you* get demoted?"

The grin on Al's face was louder than her chuckle. "No."

"I didn't think so." They continued through the tall grass, along the well-worn pathway leading to brilliant mountain and hillside views. Violet could feel the rush of fresh air in the breeze and it caught her off guard.

She stumbled, catching herself with the trekking pole, but Al didn't overlook the misstep. "Take it easy. We'll catch up."

Violet shook her head. "That's not it." She could hear the river. "I think my senses are overwhelmed. It's so clean out here. I can almost taste it."

"Hmm." Al thought about the observation. "Never heard anyone say it like that but I understand what you mean. That's what I love about working out here in nature."

It was only day two of the fourteen day hike and Violet thought she might prove to the team leader that she wasn't a complete novice out in the wilderness even though she kind of was.

"Don't fall again," Violet whispered right before stumbling across the patch of rocks. "Shit," she swore as she felt the stones grind into her right knee and shin.

Al was a step away, too late to prevent the fall but immediately able to offer care. "Britt," she called on her radio.

"Go boss," Britt responded.

"Trip and fall." The radio crackled. "Violet needs to stop for first aid."

"I'm alright." Violet pulled away but Al grabbed her shoulder to keep her from standing.

"Stay down," she scolded. "Let me look at it before you move."

They sat in the middle of the trail. Al knelt before Violet. They were face to face with little distance between them.

"It's only scraped," Violet said. "It'll be fine in a few minutes."

"Sit here, Violet." Al's tone left no room for questions. "I have to check it." There was nothing special in the way she ran her hand over Violet's leg, but their position was too close not to feel intimate. Al's touch was meant to ensure no debris was in the wound but as she inspected Violet's shin, the smaller woman pulled away.

"Ouch, that hurts." Violet leaned back, her hand forcing down onto a pile of stones. "Ow, that hurt too." She raised her palm and a group of rocks stuck to her sweaty skin.

"Maybe you'll sit still now," Al scolded. "You've got some little pebbles in your knee."

"In?" Violet knew she was bleeding, saw she was bleeding, but had no idea that there were rocks stuck in her skin.

"Yes, oh my gosh if you would sit still for a moment I'd be able to remove them." It was more a request than a demand but either way one of them needed to clean the wound.

"Go ahead." Violet closed her eyes as Al's calloused fingers moved across her shin.

"I'll try to be gentle." Al held Violet's calf in one hand while she rolled grain-sized pebbles from Violet's wounds. Al shrugged her backpack off her shoulder and took out a small folded bandana from the side pocket. She soaked it with water. Bit by bit, she wiped away the dirt and blood left behind by the fall. She looked up at Violet. "Hey." She saw the tears in the woman's eyes.

"It's not painful." Violet wiped the tears on her shirt sleeve. "It's embarrassing."

Al finished wiping the blood away and began fanning across Violet's knee. "There's nothing to be embarrassed about."

"What's the emergency?" Britt stopped, taking in the sight of their team leader holding their client's leg while waving over her knee. The client had tears in her eyes. If Britt didn't know Al so well she might have questioned the situation.

"Violet took a hard fall." Al wiped a smear of blood from Violet's calf.

"Ugh, does everyone have to watch?" Violet covered her face with the bend of her arm. They were a small team of five. It was impossible to avoid the curiosity and also the need for help.

"First-aid kit." PB removed it from her pack. "Do you need help?"

"Open up the gauze for me while I wash it properly." Al squirted a small packet of disinfectant on the open cuts and scrapes, wiping them with the sterile gauze PB held. It didn't take long to cover the wounds and get Violet back on her feet.

"It's so bad when I've got a trekking pole in each hand and I still fall down."

"People fall," Britt said. "I promise you, someone takes a fall on almost every trip. You just got it out of the way on day two." She pointed at PB who was buckling her backpack. "That's why we carry the kit."

"Be prepared," Greta said. "At least, that's what the scouts say."

"I wasn't a scout."

"Were any of us?" PB waved around the circle. "Last I checked it was exclusive."

"Every single one of the skills they taught were all in the handbook." Al twisted the towel before tying it to the carabiner dangling from the backpack. "I had a library card and I didn't need anyone to approve my skills."

"You were a secret boy scout?" Greta asked, with a level of enthusiasm that bordered on worship.

"I wasn't a secret anything. I was as out as I could be." Al swiped the dirt from her pants and offered Violet a hand up.

"That's no surprise either," Greta said.

"Are you going to be okay with hiking?" PB asked Violet as she positioned herself behind Greta.

"I'll be fine. It wasn't that bad." Violet stared at the blood stains on her boot. "Let's just hike and I'll let you know how I feel."

"We've got a few miles ahead of us." Al checked her watch. "If everyone's good, let's keep our cameras packed and do a double time skedaddle."

"Skeedaddle?" Violet smirked as she repeated Al's choice of word.

"Very technical hiking term. It means don't hike so slow, Violet."

Violet laughed so loud that the rest of the team turned around. "What? She's hilarious."

"Oh, yeah." Britt held a hand up in the air, waving it around like a child. "Al's an absolute laugh-riot."

"You should show that side of yourself more," Violet said, only loud enough for Al to hear.

"If I show you everything all at once, how will I keep the mystery alive?" Al joked.

"Why keep the mystery at all?"

~~~~~~~~~~~

"How's the leg?" Al asked as she picked up her pace to walk beside Violet.

"It's sore, but I think my ego hurts more," Violet admitted.

"Don't be so hard on yourself."

Violet stabbed the ground with her pole. "It was a stupid slip."

Al lifted her shirt, revealing the scar on her rib. "Cracked that sucker climbing. It happens to all of us."

"You were climbing." Violet sidestepped a fallen tree limb. "I tripped on my own feet."

"That happens, too."
~~~~~~~~~~~

Chapter Ten

"We're at site two," Britt radioed and the echo made her turn around.

"So are we," Al said as she ducked under the reserved sign roping off their pre-booked site. They'd hiked through the forest looping around into the national park's camping area. It was the one and only overnight stay that had pit toilets and rustic but usable semi-hot-water showers.

"Look at you, Violet, keeping up with the rest of us." PB was unpacking the gear for fishing and striking camp. "And with a bum leg."

Violet grinned. "It's not so bad." She patted the bandage stained with splotches of blood.

"I'm off to get water." Al grabbed the bladder and disappeared into the woods. Violet stared after her, wondering why she ran so hot and cold.

"Let's get it done, team." Britt clapped her hands together.

"We're on fishing duty for dinner." PB raised the gear and she and Greta headed toward the river.

Violet rolled the two-person tent out across the ground. She and Al had shared the tent the night before and thoughts of sleep-induced snuggles distracted her focus. The poles flexed as she fit them into the anchoring loops—this part was too easy. Her hands began to sweat as she stretched the rope ends.

Tying knots was her kryptonite, the weakness of all weaknesses, and she didn't want the team leader to pop in while she fumbled again and again.

"The tent looks right, but why can't I get these tighter?" Violet pulled her rope but it didn't hold and went slack each time she tugged it.

Britt was nearly finished with the tent that was almost twice the structure that Violet was assembling. Unlike the previous site, this site wasn't divided by the huge downed tree, so the tents would be arranged around the fire pit a little differently than they had been the night before.

Britt studied Violet's knot in the anchoring rope. "So this is the problem with your technique." She took her time demonstrating how to swoop one end around before twisting the loop over the top. She dropped on one knee, tugging the rope once to demonstrate how to take up and draw out slack to adjust the entire knot for cinching.

"Holy shit, how did you do that so fast?" Violet sat down cross-legged to study the knot.

"I've been doing this longer than almost anything." Britt demonstrated the technique again, exaggerating the loop sizes to make it easier for Violet to see.

"That's obvious." Violet relaxed her hands in her lap.

"Plus, the boss is intense about anchoring equipment, and knots save our lives when we climb."

"Yeah, I got the intensity part during evaluation week." Violet removed the rope and tried to replicate the maneuver. "Is she always like that?"

Britt leaned away, taking a moment to assess Violet's curiosity and her intention behind the question. She saw kindness in Violet's eyes but there was something else, too, and she needed to find out what Violet was really asking. "Al, well, she's a tough nut to crack but once you understand her, there's always a reason for the seriousness."

"Yep, but the hot and cold… I think I've felt more cold in the last few days."

Britt shrugged. "She had it rough at home as a kid. She's tough because of that, but when you get to know her she's ridiculously soft on the inside."

"Really?" Violet wanted to believe. Her next attempt at tying was more of a tangled mess than a cinching knot. "I think I got a little bit of that softer side when this happened." She tapped the bandage on her knee. "But it felt more like pity."

Britt cracked a smile. She'd noticed her team leader holding Violet's knee— fanning across the wound seemed like a little bit more than typical trail wound care. The two had lagged behind yesterday and earlier that morning. This was Britt's chance to probe deeper to know exactly what level of interest Violet had in her best friend Al. "It takes time to get to know her, plus she's got this new love in her life."

Violet looked up. "New love?" Clearly disappointed that there might already be someone, Vi fumbled the knot tying again. "She didn't mention a significant other last night."

"No. Well, I found her in a magazine, actually," Britt continued. "Her name is Bess and trust me, Al did not want to leave her behind for two weeks." A huge grin followed her mischievous chuckle.

Violet shook her head. What woman would let her best friend look for the love of her life in a magazine? But she was also happy to hear that someone had captured the heart of that unapproachable, tough woman. Trying to stay on task, Violet made a solid third attempt at securing the tent. "Sounds a little serious if she didn't want to leave her behind."

"Bess might be Al's first love." Britt took hold of the rope one more time. With skilled hands, she passed the working end over and around the standing part, much slower than before so Violet could copy the technique.

Violet thought about their team leader and the stories told of her adventures. By Violet's estimate, Al had to be close to thirty, so how could Bess be her first love. "Really? Her *first* love?"

"Oh for sure. Like I said, she's soft inside, so don't let that tough-girl act fool you." Britt was pleased with herself and also intrigued by Violet's reactions.

"I see my mistake," Violet said.

Britt wasn't expecting the emotional turnaround. "Mistake?"

Violet lifted the rope. After repeating her missed step in the knot tying, she had a perfectly adjustable taut line hitch. "Not bad, right?"

"Look at you!" Britt said with a slow clap as she walked around their tents. "Now repeat that six more times and you'll impress her, too." She hitched her thumb toward Al who was approaching from the forest.

"You're not finished, yet?" Al was strictly business as she dropped a bundle of firewood and set the bladder on the ground by the fire pit. She unbuckled the backpack and removed the filet knife from the mess kit.

"Britt was giving me a rope-tying lesson." Violet held up the loose end.

"Knots—again?" Al tipped the sheathed part of the blade to point at the untethered tent. From her angle, she couldn't appreciate the perfect knot on the opposite side.

"She did great," Britt said.

"Yeah, it looks like it." It was obvious from Al's stare that she saw all of the poorly-tied ropes. "We've got a few trout to filet. Maybe you can get that fire going?" She didn't wait for an answer as she disappeared back in the direction she came from.

"I'm doing my best." Violet huffed. "Why is she always so grumpy?"

It was Britt's turn to collect a pile of tinder and arrange the kindling. "She's not grumpy—she's serious."

"I get the feeling she doesn't like me very much." Violet cheered internally as she tied the third anchoring knot.

"She's got to make sure we all stay focused out here." Britt struck a match, igniting the tiny bits of dried pine needles and grass. "If she didn't want you on this trip, you wouldn't be here."

"Really?" Violet paused to let that information sink in. "So her intensity isn't directed at me?" She tied another anchoring rope a little faster this time, with less hesitation.

Britt split a log and added the smaller pieces to fuel the flashing flames. "It's not just you she's focused on. She's taking care of all of us."

"Done," Violet said as she swished the dirt from her palms. "When it comes to Alice, I'll trust you know best."

Britt looked up at her, a serious glare on her face. "Calling her by her full name is a great way to piss her off."

"Seriously?"

"Uh, yeah." Britt made no apologies for this truth. "She really hates it."

Violet tipped her head curiously, "What's the name thing all about?" She thought the question was innocent, but looking up Al's expression told her otherwise.

"It's about respecting someone's boundaries," Al said as she stepped from the forest. "Maybe we should add that to our climbing-readiness day checklist?"

"I didn't mean anything—"

Al raised a silencing finger. "I know what you were asking and it has nothing to do with this excursion." She dropped the pot filled with water and the filets beside the fire pit. "Britt, will you go and help clean the fishing site? Greta might have tangled our lines again."

"All of them?" Britt asked.

"Afraid so." Al chuckled.

"I'm on it." Britt grabbed her headlamp and disappeared into the setting darkness.

"I didn't mean anything terrible when I used your name," Violet whispered, aware that she and Al were alone again. Al prodded the logs, more aggressively than necessary, before placing the cooking pan atop the flame. Violet was prepared for silence and was startled when the other woman began to speak.

Al didn't look at her but Violet could feel the intensity in her tone. "You know, or maybe you don't know, but you're a bit much sometimes?"

"Am I?" Violet crossed her arms, defensive, despite knowing Al had every right to call out her lack of respect for a solid boundary.

"Yeah, you are."

"And you're an expert on how *much* I am?" Violet bit back.

"I'm pretty sure I'm not even close to being a novice." Al shook her head slowly. It was impossible to miss their communication impasse when the two of them snickered at the same time. She set the trout filets in the pan and placed them on the fire.

The silence that followed was an understanding of the need for space as Al poured water into the pot to boil while adjusting the fish, flipping each of the filets with more care than necessary.

Secretly, Al liked the way her full name sounded coming from the curly-haired woman, but scars didn't disappear because a person caught your eye.

Violet settled on the ground as Al finished preparing the freeze-dried rice and beans. Tonight they'd eat dinner as semi-cohesive team members, settling on the notion that maybe they could get along for the next few weeks.

~~~~~~~~~~

After a satisfying meal of fish and foraged greens, Britt and Greta washed dishes, happy to be away from the fire. Two fly rods were stored in their bags, lines untangled and wound tight,
~~~~~~~~~~

ready to use the next day. Britt had the dexterity to manage tangled fishing lines. As they returned to camp, Al, PB and Violet managed the fire in silence.

"Britt and I are enjoying the bigger tent." PB grinned. "You're still good with Greta staying with us?" she asked. She had recognized the tension between Al and Violet as she scraped the remnants on her plate into the fire.

"Everything stays as is," Al said. "Nothing needs to change."

PB nodded. "Great, since it's late and I definitely don't want to pull all of our gear out."

"It's fine." Al shifted as Violet stood.

"I think I'm going to turn in. If that's okay," Violet said. She'd been quiet while they ate, lost in replaying her side of the conversation which had escalated to more of an argument earlier.

Al was strong and guarded, and that suited the leadership role she had. What Violet wanted now was to catch more than a glimpse of the tender Alice who'd held her injured leg. That touch of care that made her feel safe when she was tearful and humiliated. Violet felt remorse about saying Alice's full name out loud but only because what little kindness she'd gained seemed to disappear back to point A.

"Goodnight, Vi." PB said the shortened version of her name mostly as a joke.

Violet didn't mind—not many people used it aside from her Aunt Eunice, who happened to be her favorite person. "Goodnight." She carried her backpack into the tent and dragged the zipper all the way around to close the door.

"Decisions about going to bed have been made I guess." Al kicked her boots out. Using her pack as a backrest, she settled in.

The evening was practically perfect for the rest of the team. A slight breeze stirred the scent of pine around their campsite and Britt stopped to enjoy the uncountable stars in the sky. "Anyone interested in taking a night hike?" Britt asked as she tucked their plates in the kitchen kit and hoisted it into the trees.

"That sounds perfect," PB said. "Let me put on some long pants and we can head toward the overlook."

"I'm in." Greta raised her hand, giggling when she realized the gesture wasn't necessary.

"Al, are you interested?" Britt asked.

"Nah, Violet's already in the tent so it's better if one of us stays here. Safety in numbers, remember."

"I remember. Don't fall asleep by the fire." Britt pointed to her friend. "We don't want toasty Al when we come back."

"You just watch the sky and I'll watch camp." Al pulled out her guide notebook. "I'll square away tomorrow's schedule."

Britt knew the schedule was set, that there wasn't a single thing that needed squaring or circling either, but she understood Al. There was a contract between them, a hierarchy out in the wild, but this hesitation seemed larger than a need to keep an eye on one of their clients.

After the rest of the team cleared out, Al sat for the longest time, watching the fire burn while fighting the childhood memories Violet had stirred. She wanted more than anything to make the pain of rejection disappear, but an instant fix was only a dream. Her head relaxed against the rucksack as she closed her eyes.

The next thing Al felt was the chill of the night air and she knew she couldn't avoid Violet any longer. She stirred the coals of the fire, breaking them apart and pouring their wash water until the pit was a steaming pile of ash. She set their lantern on the stump as a signal for the star gazers and headed to bed.

Al wanted her tent-mate to be sleeping, but as she zipped herself inside she heard a deep sigh and a hesitant whisper. "I'm very sorry, Al." Violet's short apology told a long story of regret. It was clear from the tone that Violet had spent the last hour thinking about her.

Al didn't move. She sat and unlaced her boots with more attention than necessary. She had been thinking, too. Secretly, she wanted to have a private talk with this infuriating but attractive woman. But she was tired and impatient and the last thing she wanted was another emotional battle.

"Thanks, I appreciate the apology," was all she said. She shoved the laces in her boots, palmed her sleeping bag flat and adjusted herself to rest.

"I'm not a member of whatever group of people who hurt you."

"Obviously not, but I'd appreciate it if you'd respect who I am." It wasn't a snarky request but Al hoped that Violet got the hint.

"Al, I respect who you are but I also think Alice is a beautiful name." Violet rolled toward her team leader, not in a hurry to escape the conversation but grasping that she'd once again crossed a very personal boundary.

"Maybe it's a beautiful name for someone else."

Violet paused to comment on the sadness in Al's voice. "It is beautiful for the way I see you, but I was out of line and I'm sorry if I hurt you."

Al ripped her shirt over her head roughly, revealing her sports bra. "Please, will you please just let it go for tonight." Stripped down to her shorts, she felt more naked than ever before.

"Just for tonight?" Violet rolled to face Al.

Al's face was hidden in shadow when her fragile whisper escaped. "Please."

Chapter Eleven

In the dark of night, they repeated the intimate moment. From inside her sleeping bag, Violet huddled as close to Al as she could get.

The team leader struggled to sleep, caught between the frustration of the triggering name, Alice, and the idea that this curious woman could say it with such a level of affection.

It's just a name: Alice, she thought. She lay rigid like a pole, so as not to wake Violet. She didn't want her to know how much it hurt. She never wanted anyone to know about the damage words made, about what wounds she carried on the inside. Violet had gotten deep under her skin and she didn't hate it—well, not completely—and that was the most confusing part.

Tomorrow, she would fortify her walls. She'd guard herself from the tiny powerhouse taking up space in her mind and in this compact two-person tent. Twelve days. In twelve days she'd be free of Violet Crest and she'd never have to see her again. She was the team leader—she had that power.

~~~~~~~~~~~

Al was the first one up the next morning, mostly because she'd hardly slept. She decided she'd fight the lethargy by building a fire to boil water for her revitalizing instant coffee.

"Stupid damn name," she mumbled as she filled the pot and set it over the flames. She hadn't been in this place for years: the limbo between Al and Alice, and the sound of disappointment that second syllable provoked. Feeling lost in her solitude, she poked the ground around the fire pit stones.

Violet, a delicate name for such a ferocious spitfire of a woman, she thought. *Get out of my head.* She lowered their mess kit from the trees, knowing PB's plan to make campfire
~~~~~~~~~~~

biscuits to go along with her not-so-secret anymore secret jam. She had no idea how late the rest of the team had sat stargazing on their night hike but decided she would give them another half hour to rest.

"Good morning," Violet whispered.

The sound broke Al from the downward thought-spiral she was in. "Good morning. How did you do on the ground last night?" She hooked the pot cover, checked for boiling bubbles and immediately removed it from the flame.

"I slept a little." Violet had a tin cup in her hand. "Is there a chance you're making water for coffee?"

Al smiled. "It's absolutely the first order of business this morning."

"Oh you're so wonderful. If you didn't already have a partner I might just marry you." Violet's butt landed in the dirt as she plopped beside the open mess kit.

Al reached for the cup, questioning, "I have a partner? Like for business or pleasure?"

Violet stared at Al through large brown eyes. Confused by Al's questions, she blinked hard as she released the tin cup. "Brittney says that some girl named Bess is your first love." She rested her forearms on her bent knees as she watched Al perform the mundane but suddenly very important task of making instant coffee. "So a partner for pleasure, I'd guess."

Al opened the zipper pouch containing the instant coffee. "Huh."

The sound was curious, Violet thought. Perhaps it was a pause to think or maybe she was gathering the courage to share her vulnerability. Technically this was none of her business, but since the two of them would be spending the next few weeks together hiking through the national forest, she needed to settle the undeniable attraction between them.

"Britt, the bitch." Al cursed louder than she'd intended. "She's such a pain in my ass." Al set her cup beside Violet's. "One scoop or two?" She held a measured spoonful of the dehydrated crystals over Violet's cup.

"Two, please. I think I'm gonna need caffeine today." Violet rubbed her hands together. It was mostly to calm her nerves but would also look like she was eager for the heat of the steaming cup.

"I think I'll need it too," Al returned to the task that was menial but for some reason needed her complete focus. '*Don't look at those eyes,*' she thought.

"So Bess isn't your girlfriend?"

The curiosity in Violet's tone made Al pause to look at her. The raised eyebrow was adorable, and the way the morning sunrise lit her hazy brown eyes made her smile. Al stirred the spoon distractedly to mix the dehydrated bits into the water.

"Bess isn't even a friend, technically." Al chuckled as she passed the mug to Violet.

Violet cradled the mug with both hands, eager for something to occupy her fidgeting hands. "But Britt said—"

Al shook her head, interrupting before Violet could feel the embarrassment of Britt's deception. "Bess is my new car."

"A car," Violet whispered.

"Well, not just any car. Britt is going to have a hard time hiking out of here after I take her gear and leave her behind."

"Oh, don't do that," Violet said. Her lips formed a perfect tiny puckered "O" before she blew across the top of her mug.

Al looked away, caught off guard by Violet's lips and sweet expression. She fumbled to recover the pause in conversation. "Uh, yeah. Well, she's always looking to stir up a little mischief."

"Yes, she's also adding fun to the adventure, so I don't mind." Violet took a quick sip. "Tell me about Bess."

There was a loud gasp.

"Oh shit!" Britt covered her mouth, backing away just as she was about to sneak up on Al. The aroma of instant coffee had called her to the early morning fire but now she had regrets.

"'Oh shit' is right." Al threw an empty cup at her friend.

Britt had fast hands and snatched it out of the air. "I guess you told her?"

Violet puffed another breath across her mug.

"She did and apparently I'm in love with my car." Al sat beside Violet.

"Bess is all you talk about," Britt said in defense as she mixed a mug of dehydrated coffee. "Technically, it's not a lie."

"What's not a lie?" PB asked, rubbing her eyes as she and Greta joined the rest of the team.

"Nothing," Al said. The conversation was about to become more story than she wanted to share and potentially more revealing when it came to her private thoughts about Violet.

"So we're not going to share with the rest of the family?" Britt asked, noticing the flush to Violet's cheeks.

"Come on, share!" PB set her tin cup down for a hot water fill-up.

"You two are impossible." Al looked at Greta. "You want some instant coffee?"

"Please." Greta rubbed her hands together. "Mostly to warm me a little. It got cold looking at the stars and I can't shake that chill."

"Was it chilly for you, Al?" Britt asked and all eyes returned to the team leader.

"Not until the fire went out." Al sipped her coffee.

"I see." Britt winked at Violet and the subtle flush in her cheeks escalated into a full face blush.

"You *see* nothing," Al deflected. "Aren't you supposed to help PB with breakfast?" She passed the mugs to the rest of the team.

Britt's mischievous snicker transformed into a laugh. "Yes, I jam."

"Oh hell no, you didn't just say that." PB tossed a stick at her.

Britt sidestepped, spilling a little of her coffee on the ground. "Come on, Al was going to tell us all about her new crush."

"You have a crush?" PB looked directly at Violet.

Al stepped in front of her friend, her back to the rest of the team. "They're talking about Bess!"

"Bess?" PB laughed loud enough to scare the animals in the forest and beyond. "She's a car. For fuck's sake, she's *only* a car."

Britt's gasp was louder than Al's. "She is not *only* a car."

"Perhaps the two of you can debate my love affair with Bess while you overload us with carbohydrates and sugar for the day?"

"You want us to make breakfast?" PB pointed at the fire, flicked her finger at the bag dangling in the tree and back at Britt.

"That's the plan, and we'll get water for you and for more very delicious coffee." Al carried the empty bladder, waving at Violet and Greta to follow her.

Although Al left her coffee on the rock, Violet and Greta took theirs along. There was no way they were abandoning caffeine in a warm mug that morning.

The river was less than a half mile from camp, convenient for the amount of water they'd boil for the day. Before they were five yards from the rest of the team, Greta asked, "What kind of car is Bess?"

Al smiled. She did love her car, but not like that. It was more than buying Bess new. It was more than picking exactly what features she wanted Bess to have. It was that Bess was hers and that she was going to spend the next unknown amount of years making memories with her.

"Wait." Greta grabbed Al's shoulder, spilling a bit of her coffee where they stopped on the trail. "Don't tell me. Let me guess?" She sized up their team leader, really evaluating her as a person from head to toe. This wasn't difficult at all. "You probably got something sporty. Kinda like you."

"Sporty?" Al questioned as she turned to continue their walk to the river.

Violet snickered, her eyes gleaming as she sipped from her cup. She knew what Greta was saying. Sporty, otherwise known as butch. Al was definitely a very fine masculine-presenting person.

"You know…" Greta made an awkward bicep flexing gesture. "Built for action. Sporty."

Al shook her head. This all-female team did not have the group tone she'd planned. She turned around to look at Violet and Greta. "Built for action?"

"Don't you ever look at yourself?" Greta asked.

Al kicked off her boots, rolled up her sleeves and waded into the calmest part of the moving water. "I look at myself as little as possible."

Violet's tiny gasp got Al's attention.

"You're kinda hot." Greta looked at Violet for confirmation. "I'm not wrong, right?"

Afraid to agree out loud, Violet hid behind a sip of her coffee. "Mm hmm."

"See, I'm right. So a sporty gal like you needs a gettin' around truck. You got a Ford Escape."

"What?" The horror on Al's face made Violet laugh. "Ford Escape?"

Violet shook off the idea that the woman scooping water in the middle of a river would drive the car of a school teacher.

"Yeah, they are kinda popular." Greta sipped her coffee.

"Bess could never be a Ford." Al waded to shore carrying the full bladder of water.

"Is it a pickup?"

"*She* is not a pickup." Al paused to watch the river flow, admiring the morning sunshine dancing atop the ripples of water. "A pickup is definitely not my style."

"Okay, so not a pickup. Did you get one of those fancy new electric ones?"

"Ugh, there's no way." Al shook her foot before sticking it in her boot. "You've seen my backpack. Too much gear for that." She dropped down to lace her boots.

"She's a Subaru," Violet blurted. "Bess is a Subaru."

Al smiled as she stood, touching her finger to the tip of her nose. "Ding, ding, ding." She pointed at Violet. "We have a winner, folks. Tell her what she's won."

"The company is very supportive," Violet added.

Greta scrunched her nose. "What does that mean?"

Violet leaned in to whisper in Greta's ear, loud enough for Al to hear, "It's a lesbian thing." It was the first time Al and Violet openly spoke about what they'd danced around for the last two days.

"That I wouldn't know about." Greta shrugged.

"It's super top secret." Violet was feeling playful, happy after learning that the team leader might be single, and maybe, if she could stop tripping over her feet, and her mouth, they could get to know one another better.

"Not so top secret anymore." Al chuckled. As she led them back to camp, she thought about the day ahead and the curious moments Violet would inevitably weave into it. She hoped for gorgeous views with sudden photo opportunities, and a pace slow enough to appreciate Violet's free spirit.

Chapter Twelve

As they walked back to camp, Al heard a deep voice screaming. Someone was in pain. It was a sound she'd heard on the trail a few times before.

"What was that?" Greta asked. She turned in the opposite direction from their campsite.

"It sounded bad," Violet said.

"Take this back to camp." Al passed the water bladder to her team members, felt for the radio on her belt and rushed off toward the sound.

"What just happened?" Greta turned toward Violet. "What do we do?"

"Take this back to the team." Violet attempted to lift the water container. "Shit, this is heavy." She waved Greta closer. "Help me with this."

They carried the weight together as they shuffled side-by-side up the path toward their campsite.

By the time they arrived, PB was standing at the edge of camp communicating with Al by radio. "Copy that," she said, her tone serious.

"There was loud yelling—" Greta began to explain.

"Some guy fell from a drop off," Britt said as she pulled the pan from the flames. "Al's there."

"She took off while we were getting water."

"A ranger's been notified and we'll wait here for Al's instructions," PB instructed.

They set up to boil water as PB prepped for the morning meal. Seconds later, their team leader entered camp.

"I need the medical kit." Al huffed, breathy from running. She didn't say anything else as she grabbed a climbing rope and harness.

Britt reacted without hesitation. She thumped the canvas first-aid kit over her shoulder, grabbed a harness, and she and Al disappeared into the forest.

"Whose blood was on her shirt?" Violet asked.

"Not sure whose blood it was, but it looks like she'll probably need our hands."

PB grabbed hold of Greta who stood frozen in place, obviously in shock. Violet hop-ran behind them, cursing her scuffed knee as she chased the quick moving team. They stumbled down a fresh cut trail until they hit the narrowest part.

The sheer drop made Violet hug the rocky cliffside. A climbing rope lay anchored to the opposite rock wall leading to what seemed like nowhere.

"Down here." Al's voice broke through the tall brush.

PB stopped and dropped to her belly. "What the hell?" she yelled. "How did you get back down there so fast?"

Violet leaned over and her eyes locked on the site of two guys huddled over a third. From her angle, a head wound and a broken arm were the cause of the ear-splitting shrieks coming from below. The deformed and twisted angle of the arm caused Greta to vomit. Violet almost lost it herself as Al and Britt attempted to support the injury.

"What do you need from me?" PB yelled.

Al looked up with a smear of blood on her cheek. "His head is a bloody mess. I can't hold pressure on it. I'm about to stabilize his arm and try to bring him up."

"We're going to do a simple extraction," Britt explained to the men beside her. The lack of safety gear made it clear they were inexperienced hikers out for an ill-advised adventure.

Al was cautious as she wrapped the arm between two parts of a separated trekking pole. Greta leaned forward to puke again.

"Come over here." PB moved the woman out of the way so she could help Al and Britt.

Violet closed her eyes. She wasn't affected by blood but for some reason the gagging sound coming from Greta made her throat tense. "Do you need me to help pull him up?"

Britt nodded. She focused on anchoring the belay ropes to the rocks along the trail. Together, the team would guide the wounded man out of the ravine.

"All you have to do is pull when I tell you to pull, and when they get him to the top, I'll help them with the rest." Britt held both of Violet's hands, making direct eye contact. "Got it?"

Violet nodded. "Got it."

For the next twenty minutes, the team grunted and groaned their way to the top. Greta was barely able to help, as she was so caught up by the sight of blood and vomiting, and stayed out of the way.

Al kicked herself over the top as Britt and PB laid the man on the ground. The wounded man, unable to say his name, was obviously incapable of hiking out of the forest. His friends were equally as slow as they crawled up onto the trail. It was obvious to Al that all three men were experiencing different levels of shock.

"Guys," Al yelled to get their attention. "I can't carry your friend on my own." She barked orders at them as Britt dismantled the hastily-placed climbing rigs and tossed them toward the still vomiting Greta.

PB had already run ahead, and by the time they dragged the man into camp, they could hear and see Park Services vehicles approaching.

"Head wounds are a nightmare," Al said as she helped settle the man in the rescue basket.

"The bleeding slowed when we were able to apply pressure," Britt added. "But getting him to the top took a few minutes longer because his buddies were useless."

"Let's get him out of here," the ranger yelled to his partner.

"Are you with him?" the ranger asked Al, assuming by her actions that this was her team.

"No, these two guys are." Al pointed at the dazed men standing helplessly beside the ranger's four-wheeler.

"Good job with him," the ranger said before starting the engine and moving slowly through the groomed trails. The team watched silently as the rangers disappeared. The injured man howled as they traversed the rough terrain.

"Did that really just happen?" Greta wiped her mouth on her sleeve.

Violet picked up the coffee cup, rinsed out the dirt and filled it with water. "Take a drink." She handed it to Greta, who walked toward the trees. She swished her mouth a few times, spitting into the grass.

"Is everyone else alright?" P.B. asked.

The four of them stood in silence, each taking in the appearance of their team leader. Al's shirt was covered in the stranger's blood.

"You should go clean up." Britt held out a towel as she tapped her friend's shoulder.

Al held her hands in front of her, noticing the blood. "Yeah, I probably should." She crossed the campsite to head to the river. "We don't want to attract unwanted things."

"I'm going with her." Violet took the towel from Britt and walked away, unconcerned with PB or Britt's reaction.

Chapter Thirteen

Violet followed her team leader through the trees. Al was quick as she chose a weaving path to a new location farther away from camp. This shoreline was rocky, absent of sand for surefooted walking, and Violet was careful as she approached to stand beside Al. The river moved fast across the rocks.

"Are you okay?" Violet asked.

Al was fully aware of her surroundings, but also reserved about her current situation. She didn't want a paying client to see anything other than the powerful, confident persona she'd constructed. She looked down at herself. She was covered in a stranger's blood, with this intriguing woman standing beside her. Violet was offering kindness, without strings, but in this moment of vulnerability, Alice struggled against the weakening barrier.

"I'll be fine." Al dropped to a knee, fumbling with the lace on her boot.

Violet noticed her trembling hands. "Shh, sit down." For the first time in nearly three days, Violet touched her team leader. With gentle hands, she wrapped her fingers around Al's bicep. The muscle tensed, not from fitness but from the adrenaline rush that would soon cause a physical crash. Violet wouldn't be able to move Al if that physical collapse happened by the river's edge.

"I'm going to help you with your bloody clothes." Violet's fingers moved toward the buttons on Al's long-sleeved shirt.

Al stilled Violet's fingers. "No, don't." She kicked out of her boots, slid her butt down the face of the rock and lowered herself, fully clothed, into the water. She didn't dare step beyond her knees, certain the current and her sudden exhaustion would carry her downstream.

"What are you doing?" Violet asked as Al sank to let the icy water wash over her skin. "Oh, an ice bath. How frigid," Violet said to absolutely no one as she stood by the rushing water waiting for whatever Al did next.

A shirt came flying towards the shore, followed by a pair of pants that zipped off into shorts. The sports bra landed at Violet's feet and she looked up to see Al dunk her head below the water.

Violet turned her back to give Al the privacy she deserved.

Al popped up to see Violet's backward position. It seemed ridiculous. "You're not going to see any new body parts," she said, as she wiped her arms and plunged them a few times to wash away the stranger's blood.

"I know that." Violet kept her back turned. "You should have some privacy." She could hear Al sloshing toward shore.

"I'm sorry." Al was an arm's length away. "Thank you."

Violet was still holding the towel and she felt a few drops of water on her skin as Al reached to take it.

"I wasn't thinking," Al said.

Violet kept her eyes averted as one-by-one, the pile of clothes disappeared from the ground in front of her.

Al settled on the rock, wringing water from the clothes she'd rinsed in the river. "I wouldn't have done that with anyone else. Well, I would have done it with Britt or PB. God knows they've seen me naked more times than I can count."

"Really?" Violet chuckled.

"After twenty years of friendship, and the wild child I was." Al chuckled. "I hardly ever had clothes on in the summer when we were kids."

"You walked around naked?"

"You don't have to look away anymore, Violet. My shirt is on."

Violet stared at the water-soaked person sitting on the rock in front of her. The abandoned bra lay in a twisted pile with the zipped-off bottoms of Al's pants. Al looked almost relaxed, with the towel over her shoulder and her feet kicked into the swirling river water.

"I didn't walk around naked. I was in a swimming suit."

"All the time?" Violet asked. She looked at Al. Alice. The woman truly looked like the thoughtful complexity that Violet envisioned in the full name.

"I didn't have adults that engaged beyond reminding me how unnecessary I was."

"That is a horrible way to treat your child. Did they use more than words to hurt you?" Violet whispered the question, unsure she wanted an answer and more uncertain that Al would give one.

"They never hit me, if that's what you're asking, but they made sure I knew my place."

"Your place?" Violet asked.

"Where I did and didn't belong." Al rubbed the towel across her head to dry her hair. "You know." Her voice broke.

"No, please tell me." Violet sat on the rock beside the strong but vulnerable woman, wishing there was a way to take away her pain.

Al took a moment to clear her throat and second-guess what she was about to reveal. She did have a past, but it was hers. Perhaps this small but mighty woman beside her could be trusted with it, too.

"Here's the thing." Al didn't turn toward Violet as she spoke. "For most of my childhood, all I ever heard was '*Alice,* you're not good enough.'" It still hurt to voice the words, to say and hear her own name out loud. "Almost always it was '*Alice,* you could do more if you worked harder.' 'Why can't you be better?' 'Who told you that was the right way to do it?' But that last time it was '*Alice,* if you're late you better not come home.'" She stared out across the water.

Violet's gasp lingered in the space between them. Hesitant, she turned to look at Alice as she moved closer. Unaware that the rest of the world was going on around them, she said, her voice low, "And you were late."

Al's shoulders fell, answering like a vulnerable child with a defeated trembling nod.

"What did you do?"

Al shook her head, fighting back the ridiculous rush of emotion. Maybe it was coming down from the urgency of the rescue, or perhaps it was the cold water shock to her system, but it was mostly how safe she felt with the woman beside her. She looked directly into Violet's eyes, and said, "I never went home again."

Violet scooted as close as she could get without touching. "So that's why you started the Extreme Adventure Group?"

Al rubbed her hands across her thighs, appreciating the calming sensation that anchored her to the moment. The sun's heat warmed her and the light dancing across the river lit them in a fantastic golden hue. "EAG is family for Britt, PB and me, but yes, that's why I started hiking and climbing. I wanted to escape the idea that I didn't deserve a place to call home."

"Home is such a funny idea, isn't it?"

Al's snicker was bitter. "Yeah, funny."

"I haven't been around my family for almost six years," Violet shared. "I told them I was in love with a girl and, without letting me say another word, they shipped me away."

"So you don't have a place to call home, either."

"I have my aunt Eunice." Violet's smile was impossible to hide. "She took me in and gave me a family and a roof over my head until I finished school."

"Huh, and the girl?" Al scooted closer to Violet, trying extra hard not to touch her but wanting to, more than anything. "Was she worth it?"

Violet shook her head. "After everything I went through, she wasn't ready to make the sacrifices I did."

"What a bitch," Al whispered.

"Yeah, the entire situation really was."

As the water raced across the river rocks, Violet and Al arrived at a strange place of commonality. An unspoken agreement that they had parallel pasts with impossibly odd, intersecting presents.

"I'm sorry I called you by your full name," Violet said.

Al reached out to hold Violet's hand, needing in that moment to reassure her with physical touch that what she was about to say was an absolute truth. "Would you say it again?"

The request was whispered so quietly, Violet wasn't sure she'd heard it correctly. "What?"

Al squeezed the hand in hers. "Would you say my name again, please?" She tensed as a long pause of silence followed, fear setting in until she heard her name.

"Alice." Violet's voice was like an unbelievably gentle caress. Al closed her eyes, welcoming the sound of her name spoken without targeted harm or shame.

"Alice," Violet whispered again, turning to meet tear filled eyes.

With that second whisper, something inside Alice changed. Violet had found a way inside the fortress surrounding Alice's heart and for the first time in a very long time, she wanted to let someone in.

Chapter Fourteen

Al was first to enter the campsite. Violet followed close behind but didn't say much as she walked past the rest of the team and disappeared into her tent. She needed time to process everything that had happened in the last few hours.

"How you doin', boss?" PB asked, holding a pan of biscuits in her hand.

"I had a morning." Al smiled. "How are you three?"

Greta held up a steaming mug with leaves floating on top. "I'm not puking anymore."

Al chuckled. "That's perfect."

"Yeah, we've been talking about vomit for the last half hour." Britt made a gagging sound that set Greta off again.

"Please don't." Greta sipped more of the tea. Her face paled and she spilled her mug as she ran from the campsite.

"I foraged some mint," PB explained as she collected the spilled mug. "She'll need some more."

"She's been doing that the whole time?" Al asked, but her thoughts were mostly focused on the person inside the tent.

"Hasn't really stopped." Britt held up the pan. "Biscuit?" She offered Al a sliced puffy glob slathered in jam.

"Give me a minute to change and I'll be back." Al picked up her backpack and disappeared into her tent.

Violet sat on her bed roll, legs crossed with her hands limp in her lap.

Al crawled across the tent floor so they were sitting face to face. "Violet?" They were so much more than strangers now, and she couldn't pretend to ignore their new reality.

"Mm-hmm." Violet didn't want to cry, but she knew it was coming.

"I'm going to have a little group meeting."

Violet looked into Al's eyes. "Okay, I want to pack up my gear."

Al reached for her hands, holding them long enough for Violet to stop moving. "Wait, please."

The request, whispered with such kindness, broke through Violet's fragile facade.

Tears fell from Violet's closed eyes, and she sobbed so quietly that Al wouldn't have known if she wasn't watching her. This was a practiced shedding of sorrow, used over and over to protect herself from a lifetime lack of love.

Al reached to touch Violet's hand, to offer whatever comfort was appropriate in their current situation. Violet grabbed hold, squeezing as if her life was somehow tethered to the powerhouse in front of her.

"Violet?"

Violet shook her head, realizing she was crying and the death grip she had on Al. "Oh, gosh. I'm… I didn't mean to." She released Al. "I didn't hurt you, did I?"

Al smiled. "You didn't. But you're hurting and so is Greta." She reached for her backpack. "I need to change and then we are going to sit down as a team and talk." She turned around and pulled off her shirt and bra, replacing them with dry clothing. She did the same with her shorts while Violet sat in silence.

"Come out for a minute." Al unzipped the tent and held a hand to help Violet out.

The fire burned in the pit. The team hadn't made a move to break camp and Al was about to make a decision.

"Okay, everyone. This was not the morning we had planned."

"No shit." Britt said. "I'd like less blood."

"Don't say blood." Greta covered her mouth.

"Don't puke again." PB poured water into the pot to boil. It was looking like peppermint tea was the only thing cooking for this client.

Greta held up her hand. "I think I'm good."

"Like I was saying. I think we all need a break for the day. It's half over and there's no chance we can make it to the next site before dark. I'm calling in a favor and we'll stay on site for a second night. Violet, Greta, this won't affect your excursion. I'll just swap our climbing days around."

She waited for a response, which came in the form of simple head nods.

"What would you like us to do?" Britt waved between herself and PB.

"Keep camp and be support for Greta. I'll take care of Violet."

"Got it, boss." PB forced a smile.

"Greta, get some rest. Try to keep the tea down. We can't go anywhere if you're dehydrated."

"Is it bad that I want to curl up and sleep?"

"The fall was pretty gruesome." Britt said. "That dude was such a bleeder."

The sound of the word, the vision in her head, made Greta jump to her feet and run.

"I'll go this time," PB said. "I've never seen anyone react like this."

"No. It's weird," Britt said as she watched PB disappear into the woods.

Al stepped closer, whispering to Violet, "Why don't you go rest for a bit?"

Violet shook her head. "I'll be fine. Maybe I'll have something to eat. All of her puking is making me feel my empty stomach."

"That's new," Britt joked.

"Weird, I guess." Violet shrugged. "But I could definitely eat."

Al picked up the pan. "PB's special biscuits and jam."

Violet didn't hesitate as she reached for the fluffy white clump and took a huge bite. "This is so good."

"Jam girl knows her stuff." Britt took the water pot from the fire and filled Greta's mug again.

"She sure does." Violet's cheeks rose, revealing deep dimples. Al found them adorable and distracting and a little bit— *Be a professional*, she thought, turning her attention toward Greta as she stumbled back into camp.

"I think I need to sleep." Greta held her stomach as she shuffled toward her tent.

"I'll take her some tea and settle her in," PB said.

"I think there's something wrong with me." Greta collapsed on the ground.

"What the hell?" Britt yelled.

Greta missed hitting the campfire rock by inches as the impact of her body created a puff of debris. Violet was closest to her and rolled Greta away from the fire. She listened for a breath. "She's breathing."

"Is that blood?" Al dropped to her knees to look at the red smudge.

"It's jam from Violet's hand," Britt said.

"Oh, sorry." Violet wiped her hands on her pants before placing two fingers against Greta's carotid artery. "She has a pulse but it seems really fast."

"This isn't from seeing blood." Al's hands moved over the woman's body, checking her bare skin for a sign of injury.

PB removed Greta's boots, and when she pulled down the sock on her left foot she saw the bite. "Is this a snake?" There were two puncture marks located inches above Greta's ankle bone.

"Fuck, it is." Al looked at PB. "Did she say anything about a bite?"

"No," PB said as she looked at Britt.

"She didn't say anything." Britt tore at the backpack for the first-aid kit. "Here."

"When did this happen?" Al opened the bag. "Let's assume the worst and say rattlesnake."

"We would have known if she got bitten." Britt switched her hand radio to the park frequency and began a calm relay of what little information they had.

"I'm using the tourniquet." Violet removed the nylon strap, securing it around Greta's leg.

"No tourniquet." Al took the wrap off. "We don't know what it is or what will happen if there is venom and we isolate it." She squeezed a pack of antiseptic liquid on the wound and wiped it clean.

"This isn't good. Could it be a scorpion?" Violet asked as she noticed another puncture below the ankle bone.

"At this point, without her help, there's no way to know. Keep the area clean." Al pulled out a permanent marker from the bag. Making note of the time, she wrote it on Greta's skin along with tracing the bite locations. She covered the wounds with gauze.

PB came with Greta's sleeping bag. "We can carry her out using this."

"The ranger says they're still dealing with the wounded hiker but we can meet Fire and Rescue at the Aspen Fork trailhead," Britt relayed. "I told them we'd start carrying her."

"Let's go." PB rolled the unconscious woman on her side.

"Wait," Al said. She spread the sleeping bag on the ground and tugged the zipper with extra care until the bag was open. "Fuck." She jumped back.

"Baby rattler," Britt said. She kicked the dead snake toward the fire pit.

"Here's our answer." Al picked up the dead animal by the tail and tossed it into the empty pot. She took the sleeping bag and shook it a few more times. When she was satisfied there weren't additional snakes inside, she threw the sleeping bag to the ground beside PB who bundled Greta onto it.

With a woman on each corner, the team picked up the unconscious Greta to carry her out.

"Are we good?" Al asked, looking at each of them.

"Let's go." PB tugged forward, certain time was not on their side. They had no idea when the snake bite occurred and how long the venom had been pumping through Greta's system.

The terrain of the hiking trail seemed completely different as they raced to the trailhead. The canopy of trees created shade but did not protect them from the ferocity of the afternoon heat.

Violet was scared and pumped with adrenaline as she had to take two steps for every one of the long-legged EAG team members. She was keeping up but she could see the blood on her own knee where yesterday's wounds hadn't yet begun to heal. This was turning out to be a trip to remember.

"We're almost there." Al saw the marker pointing toward Aspen Fork. Greta was moaning.

"She's going to hurl again," Britt yelled.

They lowered the makeshift carrier to the ground and before they could help, Greta was rolling over and vomiting in the grass.

"How can she still be throwing up?" Violet asked.

"We need to keep moving." Al ignored the question as she grasped her corner. "Ready? On three." She counted and together they lifted Greta and moved.

Violet watched the feet of the woman in front of her, trying to keep pace with someone who had twice her physical ability.

The EMT was running toward them, intersecting a few meters from the trail head.

"Snakebite?" he asked, walking alongside their makeshift stretcher.

The team was silent as Al answered. "Little rattler. It was in her sleeping bag."

The ambulance was parked to block bystanders from viewing the scene. Their stretcher was locked in position, ready to care for Greta.

"Snakebite," the EMT yelled and his second tore at Greta's sleeping bag to gain access to her wound sites. He cut the bandage away.

"Looks like multiple bites." He noticed the marker notes and the expansion of swelling beyond the original lines. "We need to do this on the move."

Not a second was wasted as they buckled Greta to the rolling cot and pushed it into the back of the ambulance. The lights zippered back and forth, bouncing off the bodies of the rest of the EAG team.

The ranger pulled Al aside. "Are you sure it was a rattlesnake?"

"Positive." She held her fingers ten inches apart. "It couldn't have been much bigger than this.

"Stay at your site and I'll come talk with you later."

Al shook his hand. "We'll be there another night. With only one hiker we'll have to figure out our next steps."

The ranger pulled away with the ambulance and Al took a moment to assess the ragged-looking team. They were clearly exhausted, physically and emotionally, and she wondered if she appeared half as bad outwardly as she felt inside. "Let's head back," she said.

"Will they let us know how she is?" Violet asked, watching until the last possible moment for the lights and sirens to fade.

Al waited for Violet to look at her. "A park ranger will come and talk with us later."

"Will she be…" Violet didn't know how to ask the question. "Is she going to…"

"We won't know anything and it's better not to guess."

"But you've seen snake bites like that?" Violet stopped walking.

PB was serious when she said, "Rattlers can kill ya, and who knows how long she's gone untreated."

"Hey," Al interrupted. "Let's send positive thoughts, okay?"

"Sure," Violet whispered. "Positive thoughts and skilled medical hands."

"Yeah, skilled medical hands," Britt agreed as they began the slow hike back to camp.

Chapter Fifteen

"Here's the deal," Al said as she sat across from Violet. "We've had a hell of a day."

They were a ragged group as they sat around the campfire. PB's face was smeared with dirt. Britt's shirt was wet with sweat and the bandage on Violet's injured leg had patches of leaking blood. This was not the trip they'd set out to have a few days ago.

Britt chuckled. "Way to downplay a situation, boss." She tossed her hat over her knee.

"As I see it, without the original team, we're going to have a completely different experience." Al's focus was on Violet. "This isn't what you signed up for."

Violet forced a smile. "If you think about it for a minute, this *is* what I signed up for."

Al started to argue.

"Wait, hear me out." Violet held up a finger. "I filled out so many waivers and have two insurance policies. I signed up for this knowing there were risks."

Britt snickered as she pointed at the logo on her hat. "It does say 'extreme'." She tugged the cap over her sweat-soaked hair.

"That's right," PB said. "It says adventure, too."

"I know the name of our own damn company." Al poked the log in the fire. "Violet is the only client and she should get the full adventure."

"I'm not complaining," Violet said. "Where else can a novice hiker like me get a one-to-three ratio with experts like all of you?"

"You know, flattery will get you very far in this group." Britt threw her arm around Violet's shoulder.

"Thanks, that's good to know." Violet smiled and the slight hitch before she giggled made Al look up.

"Decision's made." PB smacked her hands together. "Right, Al?"

Al frowned, feeling put on the spot by her team. She wanted more time to think—more time to make a better plan—but the hope in Violet's eyes was impossible to fight.

"I guess we are continuing," Al said.

"Yay!" PB clapped.

Britt tugged Violet closer. "I knew she couldn't leave this trip half-finished."

Al unzipped the pocket on her shorts. "If we plan to keep this itinerary as is"—she flipped through her notebook—"we'll stay here for one more night."

"That means foraging and fishing," Britt said.

"Yep," Al agreed. "You want to fish with me?" she asked Violet.

"Can I lay down for a bit?" Violet asked, hesitant to request a break after fighting so hard to stay out for the rest of the planned trip.

"We're all taking some down time." Al said. "Tie up the bags, spread the coals and everyone lays down to rest."

"Can I request a sweep for critters?" Britt asked. "I'm still not sure where that little fucker came from and I sure as hell don't want to repeat today's events."

"Yep, let's take care of that now."

It took less than ten minutes to empty both tents and go through their bed rolls. Satisfied it was clear to rest, Britt set an alarm on her watch for herself and PB while Al did the same.

"Let's take two hours. See where we are and make plans for a meal."

PB was already climbing into the tent when Britt replied, "Try and close your eyes, boss."

"I'm pretty sure the best I can do is lay down."

"From you, that's a win." Britt smiled.

Violet stared at the fire, mesmerized by the dancing flames. She was trying not to think about anything but it felt like everything kept rushing in.

"We should take care of this." Al pointed at the blood on Violet's leg.

"It doesn't hurt." Violet's voice was just above a whisper.

Al put the water on to boil and walked away, not far from camp but enough to gather what was hiding in the tree. She returned with a closed hand, clearly having collected something from nature.

"Juniper berries." She held her open palm to Violet.

Violet leaned closer to sniff. "I love that scent."

Al smiled. "It might be one of my favorites." She reached for a cup and set it between them. She pulled the multi-tool knife from her pocket and began mashing the berries.

"Are you using your skills to make me better?" Violet realized that Al was about to turn the berry mash into a natural antiseptic.

"Hmm, make you better?" Taking more attention than necessary, Al mixed the mash into a little pile in the cup. "If you were any better, it'd be impossible to be near you."

"Oh." Violet blushed.

Al poured a small amount of water over the berries. "I didn't mean it like that." She was working hard not to look at Violet.

"I'm pretty sure I know what you meant."

Al chuckled. "I'm glad to hear that, because I feel a little out of my body right now." She stirred her mixture, using the water's heat to extract the medicinal elements of the berries.

"Alice," Violet whispered, knowing exactly how to get the woman to stop and look at her.

Al closed her eyes, feeling confused by the way this woman could twist her inside. Her heart and soul warred against what was and what could be if only she'd let this frustrating woman in.

The touch to her forearm was feather light. "Alice."

Al looked up into beautiful eyes staring back at her with hope and courage. "This might hurt a little."

Violet demurred. "I don't think it will."

Al fought her grin as she unwrapped a new square of gauze and dipped it in her juniper-berry tea. Her other hand trembled as she held Violet's leg steady. The dried blood turned liquid, smearing as she wiped the wounds.

Violet winced when Al cleaned the largest gash. "Sorry."

"It's okay, that's the worst one."

Al folded the gauze over, dipping it again. "Okay?" she asked before touching.

"It's okay."

This doctoring continued with slow, purposeful touches until Al was satisfied the wound was clean. "Most of these tiny ones are scabbed. They look good." She blew a gentle breath to dry the berry water. Violet's skin pebbled with tiny goosebumps that made Al grin.

"Uh, what's happening here?" Britt asked as she walked up on what looked like another intimate leg-holding scene.

Al panicked. "Snake bite."

"What?" Britt gasped and leaned in for a closer look.

Violet giggled at the two of them. It was awkward: Al blowing on her naked leg while Britt tried to figure out what was happening. "It is not a snake bite," she said.

"She needed the wound cleaned," Al explained, still holding on tightly to Violet's calf.

"Uh-huh." Britt grabbed her canteen from the rock and walked back to her tent. "You need some rest, boss," she said before disappearing inside.

"Snake bite?" Violet questioned with a giggle.

"I panicked," Al apologized, embarrassed that her thoughts were obvious to Britt.

"You're taking care of me." Violet touched the hand on her leg. "There's no reason to panic."

Al let go of the leg so she could open the waterproof wound-dressing package. She applied the covering with a gentle touch. "You should be okay to get that wet."

Violet covered it with her hand. "It feels better. Thank you."

"You're welcome." Al zipped the first-aid kit and returned it to the backpack. She tied all of the bags together and hoisted them into the air. There were five bags now but only four team members. She'd have to deal with that later.

"We should get some rest." Al pointed to their tent.

"Yes, I'm actually kind of exhausted."

Al nodded as she held a hand to help Violet stand. "That'll make it easier to fall asleep." She reached to open the zipper doorway.

Violet crawled inside and spent more time than necessary flattening out the ripples in her sleeping bag. She had so many things to say, worries and fears, but most of all she wanted to know exactly what Alice was thinking. She laid on top of her sleeping bag.

"After everything we've been through this morning, you must be tired," Violet said.

Al spent more time unlacing her boots than was necessary, trying to avoid conversation. Her defenses were down, not only from the emergency climb and a snake bite but from the unexpected way she was affected by Violet's injured leg. "I'm more worried than tired," she whispered. "Greta didn't look so good."

"Can you die from a rattlesnake bite?" Violet thought she knew the answer but asked anyway.

"You can, especially if it isn't treated right away." Al rolled onto her back, tucking her hands beneath her head. "She was pretty sick. We'll have to wait and see."

Violet turned to look at Alice. "You don't strike me as a 'wait and see' kind of person." She spoke softly, aware that there wasn't much space between their tent and the other, but hoping for privacy to talk. She was having feelings, whether attached to the drama of the day or to the gentle way Alice cared for her.

"I don't sit still very often." Al rolled to her side, immediately feeling the full power of the brown eyes focused on her.

"Have you ever been still enough to fall in love?" Violet asked.

Alice didn't move. She didn't say a word as she stared at the woman lying in front of her. The question was bold, extremely personal, and she thought Violet had guts to ask.

"Was that inappropriate?" Violet whispered.

Al pushed up to rest on her hand. "A little bit."

"Will you answer it anyway?"

Al sat up, feeling the most vulnerable she'd been in a long time. She didn't fear heights, or distance, or even diving into deep icy mountain waters, but she protected her heart like nothing else in her life—that soulful connection she kept from everyone but PB and Britt.

"Is that a no?" Violet asked, continuing to take all of the risks to further the conversation.

"Did anyone ever tell you you're kinda pushy?"

"My auntie, but she mostly says that to make me feel good about myself." Violet's smile was so big that her dimples crushed any chance Al had of avoiding an answer. "So, when it comes to romance. Have you ever let someone love you?"

"Not that way, no," Al said. There was no emotion in the response. No regret or discontent, only the absolute truth.

"Never?" Violet was intrigued. The six-foot tall woman in front of her was so much larger than a dream. Whatever the gauge for attractiveness was, Al was physically strong, emotionally controlled, and—now with the explanation of Bess —she was quite possibly available.

"Love complicates everything." Al didn't mean for it to sound harsh, or to put the smaller woman off, but for most of her life, love was a pathway to pain. As curious as she was about Violet, she needed to maintain a safe distance.

"How old are you?" Violet asked.

Al chuckled. "How old do you think I am?"

Violet wrinkled her nose. "I've been trying to do the math."

Al chuckled. "You think I'm so old that you need a calculator?" She picked at the loose thread on her sock.

"Well, Britt and PB said you met when you were eight, and started climbing at eleven, and got licensed at eighteen or nineteen, and EAG is ten years old, so you have to be close to thirty."

"Not only are you a curious photographer, but a detective, too."

The humorous response put Violet at ease. "They go hand in hand, don't you think?"

"I suppose they do," Alice said.

"Am I close?"

Al nodded. "I'll be thirty in a few months."

"You're an impressive thirty." Violet smacked herself internally for the lameness of her statement.

"Thanks." Al tipped her chin and grinned. "I don't have any milestones to calculate for you."

"You do have my birthdate on three of the dozens of forms I filled out to be here."

"You want me to get up and do research?"

"Twenty-three," Violet interrupted.

Al smiled. "Worried about my math skills?"

Violet's arm began to fall asleep so she rolled onto her back. "Honestly, I don't think I have to worry about any of your skills, Alice."

"Oh." Al felt the full force of the innuendo as her full name lingered in the air.

"Exactly my point." Violet opened the zipper on her sleeping bag and stuffed herself inside. "Thank you for today." She pushed herself forward, planted a kiss on Al's cheek, and laid down.

Al touched the spot of the kiss, stunned by Violet's bravery. "You should try and get some sleep," she said.

"So should you." Violet positioned herself so she could see her team leader and closed her eyes.

Al laid atop her bedroll. "You might have made it extremely difficult for me to accomplish a moment of rest."

"Give it a try, Alice. You're pretty good at everything you do."

Al drew in a breath, releasing it through inflated cheeks. Violet was the opposite of everything she'd expected. She was quirky and impetuous but gutsy enough to take a chance. Al rubbed her cheek, thinking she might find that same courage and let Violet in.

Chapter Sixteen

"Hey, boss." Britt hit the pole of the tent to wake up the people inside but Al wasn't sleeping.

"What's going on?" Al asked quietly through the fabric of the tent wall.

"The park ranger's here."

Which one, Al thought. She turned to see Violet's wide brown eyes staring back at her. "Did you sleep at all?" she asked.

Violet shook her cocooned head and whispered, "No."

"Come outside with me and we can hear what the ranger has to say." Al sat and pulled on her boots before scooting out of the tent.

"Hadley." The ranger offered his hand in greeting.

"Hey." Al shook his hand. "Tell me you've got some good news for us?"

He removed the notepad from his pocket, flipping halfway through to the scribbles on a page. "Ms. Finch, your injured team member is stable at Cliffside Urgent Care. The ER team confirmed your assumption of a snakebite, and your observations gave them the ability to begin immediate treatment."

"Oh, wow." Violet stood behind the team members and her gasp got everyone's attention.

"She'll be alright. She's stable." The ranger directed his assurances at Violet.

"What do you need from us?" Al asked, hoping to move the conversation, and the rest of the team, along.

"We're requesting that you stay on site for one more night so we can contact you if we need more information," he said. "You're welcome to move on with the rest of your itinerary any time after noon tomorrow."

Al nodded. She'd already made plans to remain on site to calm the team after the hiker's fall. The real issue was what to do with the single paying client who Al found more than a little interesting. "Got it," she said. Britt and PB nodded.

"I appreciate your cooperation." The ranger turned and disappeared down the trail.

Al studied the group, keeping a close eye on the way Violet was processing what had taken place. It was time to switch back into leader mode. "Okay, campers, let's make a new plan." She picked up two pieces of wood and set them in the fire pit. "I've been thinking about how to salvage what's left of this trip." She pointed at Violet. "Since you're the paying client, I'm giving you a chance to take advantage of the rest of the team's talents."

Violet grinned. "Talents?"

"Yes. Britt here is almost the best climber. PB is a very close third." The guides looked at each other and glared at their team leader.

"I suppose you're number one?" Britt shook her head, her snicker an obvious sign that they'd had this debate before.

"Obviously." Al poked the logs, rolling them over to catch fire.

"If I'm taking advantage of team talents, does that mean I get to build my own adventure?"

Al chuckled. "Something like that."

"Can we climb a little bit more than we hike?" Violet asked.

"Climbing was on the agenda for tomorrow. I'll adjust and we can add a few more days."

Britt interrupted. "Climbing will never be a hardship for any of us."

"Hell no." PB held up a hand and Britt slapped it.

"Let's talk about"—Al looked at her watch—"dinner." She laughed. "I guess we spent the best part of this day already."

"More fishing?" PB asked.

"Can I go this time?" Violet looked hopeful.

Al looked at PB. "You up for some lessons?"

"Can I turn it over to Britt?" PB said. "I did the last two and I'm so tired of untangling those lines."

"Hell no, we want to eat, don't we?" Britt joked.

Al laughed. "I'll teach, and why don't you two forage a side dish, just in case."

"We can do that." PB seemed happy to walk in the forest while Al tried to teach their worst knot-tying client how to fish using a fly rod.

"Sounds like enough of a plan." Al removed the fishing gear from the backpack and picked up the cooking pot to carry their catch home in. "Let's go play in the water, Violet."

Violet clapped her hands. "I love playing in the water."

They hiked along the edge of the river in the opposite direction of their morning swim. The shoreline was a combination of tall grass, rocks and fallen trees, and an occasional patch of sand and pebbles. It was clear by the way Al studied the water that she was searching for something in particular.

"What are you looking for?" Violet asked.

"Fish." Al held a finger to her lips, whispering, "We need to be quiet and still while we watch the water."

"For fish," Violet whispered.

"Yes."

"Under the water." Violet chuckled.

"It's a trick, you see." Al leaned in to Violet, putting an arm close enough to guide their eyes toward what she was looking for. "See the way the water hangs right there?"

"Where it looks like a little pool?"

"Yes, exactly," Al said as she sat on the rocky shore.

"The fish are in there?"

Al removed the pieces of the fishing pole from the bag and assembled it into the ten-foot length. "I'm hoping all of our fish for dinner are in there." She handed a drawstring pouch to Violet. "Will you remove the reel for me?"

Violet tugged the bag open. "The line is as thick as twine. How does that work?"

"This part of the line floats on the water," Al explained. "This fine line holds the fly, which will sink below the surface. "

"That's neat." Violet understood fly fishing more than she was letting on but watching Al so unguarded was the highlight of her day.

"It is very neat." Al slipped the fishing reel into the handle of the pole, locking it in place. "Now that we've built the pole, we need to figure out what those swimming suckers are hungry for."

"How do we do that?" Violet leaned closer to see what was inside the little plastic box in Alice's hands.

"Do you like bugs?"

"Not particularly," Violet said.

"Flip that rock over," Al said as she turned one over by her own feet.

"And we are looking for?"

"It's simple, really." Al pointed to the surface of the river. "I don't see a lot of insects flying over the water, so they'll probably be hungry for something else." She reached for a squirmy-looking wriggly grub. "Maybe this." She held it up for Violet to see.

"Okay, gross." Violet turned a rock over.

"Don't worry, we aren't using this." Al opened the plastic case. "I'm going to compare it to what's in here."

"Those are typical flies for this area?"

"Now you're getting it." Al released her live insect and returned the rocks to their previous location. "We are going to see if this little slimy thing is what our dinner wants for lunch."

"Now what?"

Al handed the fly to Violet. "Hold this while I run my line through the pole and tie the fly on."

Violet watched, captivated by Al's process of setting up her pole. Al tucked the rod and reel under her arm so she could attach the fly lure.

"This is where knot tying is a must." Al smiled at Violet.

"I'm getting better," Violet said.

"I can see you're trying. That's the only reason you're here."

Violet leaned back, getting a closer look at the woman in front of her. "Are you serious?"

"I'll joke about a lot of things, but never the safety of my team, and definitely never about the skills necessary to protect us." Al turned to look at her.

"So you're saying you've been so mean because you wanted me to work harder?"

"Have I been mean?" Al was serious.

"You're kidding, right?"

Al stopped working on the fishing rod so she could give Violet her full attention. "I'm sorry if I've been difficult with you."

"You have—," Violet paused. "PB has been hilarious and Britt is an unbelievable teacher, but you…" She hesitated. They were finally having a heart-to-heart moment and she didn't want to break the connection.

"Yes? What about me?" Al raised her eyebrow.

Violet stared at the pool of water. "You've been helpful but not in a way that makes me feel like I'm part of the team. You've kept me—I don't know—away, maybe."

Al knew she had, but it wasn't out of dislike; it was out of too much like altogether. "Maybe I have."

Violet covered Alice's hands. "Why?"

"I have my reasons." Alice didn't look at Violet, knowing without a doubt if their eyes met she would have no defense against them.

Violet pushed. "I kissed you."

Al shook her head. "I was there, remember?"

Violet pushed harder. "I'd like to do it better next time."

Al cleared her throat, adjusting her hands so that Violet could see what she was holding. "We need to tie this fly on."

"Of course we do," Violet said, disappointed but hopeful that the crack she saw was the first sign that Al would let her in.

"I'm going to use a simple technique. Watch and then I'll let you try." Al proceeded to show Violet the simple way to twirl the line and thread it through the loop created by that twirl. The technique for tying a clinch knot was all fingertips.

"You made it look easy," Violet squeaked.

"I've tied this knot thousands of times." Al used the tiny clippers to cut the fly off so Violet could try.

"I think this is trickier than you made it out to be." Violet twirled but when she released pressure on the line it balled up on itself. "I swear knots are my kryptonite." She passed the tangle to Al.

"Let me show you again."

Violet stopped Al. "Why don't you tie it on and fish. I'll get the next one." Her dimples appeared and Al figured there was no way to win this particular fight.

"That sounds like a good plan." Al tied the fly to the end of the line. "Now that we have this"—she held up the lure—"we need to get it over there." She pointed to their calm pool of water trapped against the river's edge.

"Sounds easy enough," Violet said. "What do I do?"

"You have two choices." Al stepped close to the water, pulling the line from the reel and spooling it on the wet ground. "One is to stand very close to me and the other is to stand far away."

"Those are the choices?" Violet seemed confused.

"Come here." Al scooped the woman behind her, close enough so she could see exactly how she was fishing. "I'm letting the line float downstream."

"Okay." Violet's height difference made their positions complicated as Al turned to adjust the pole.

"Next, I want to flip my pole to cast the line out." Al jerked the pole's tip, the action so smooth that it whipped the line a few yards ahead of the pool they were aiming for.

"That's pretty impressive," Violet said.

"Don't let the rest of the team know, but this is my secret addiction." Al felt a tug on the line and gave the pole a little jerk.

"Did you get one that quickly?"

Al shook her head. "Never that easy. We caught a rock." She repeated the flip action, casting the fly further upstream this time.

"So fishing is your secret addiction?"

"Shh, it's not a secret if you tell everyone." Al chuckled. The next tug on the line was a definite strike.

"Was that a bite?"

"Yep." Al jerked the pole sharply, feeling the weight of a fish against it. She held the line tightly as she pulled, drawing in an arm's length to pool at her feet again. Her hat tipped as she stepped one foot into the water.

Violet was caught up in the action, studying Al's arms while at the same time watching the fish flip out of the water and shake off the hook.

"Did it just get away?"

"It did." Al laughed. "Now the game is really on." Al pulled her hat back in place. "Stay close or you're likely to end up on the receiving end of the hook."

Violet was careful as she watched Al flip the line out. "I get a feeling that you're making this look easy."

"Fishing isn't complicated." Al watched her line, giving attention to Violet's curiosity at the same time. "But there is technique. What you're seeing is a lifetime of trial and error." She got another hit on the line. "And feeding a rumbly tummy."

Violet laughed. "And still kinda badass."

Al pooled the line at her feet, stepping forward and back as she fought to keep tension and land the fish. Her pole tip was close to the water's surface, zigging back and forth until the fish was close enough to grab.

"I've got it." Violet's hands were in the water, fearlessly grasping hold of the trout. "Look at that." She held the fish with two hands, struggling to keep her grip as it fought to return to the river.

"Nicely done." Al reached to remove the hook. "Do you know how to filet?"

Violet shook her head. "I know how to eat a filet."

Al laughed as she incapacitated the fish and laid it in the pot. "I'll teach you that next." She rinsed her hands and returned to the river's edge. "Are you ready to try?"

"Maybe you should catch a few more, just in case I 'Greta' the line."

"'Greta' the line?" Al asked.

Violet made a balling motion with her hands. "You know, tangle it into a mess."

"That's funny." Al smirked. "I'll catch a couple more and then it's your turn to 'Greta' the line."

Al cast out a few more times with no luck. Although Violet was ready to fish, she was captivated by the rhythm and calming energy of Al's actions.

"I think we should move down river a little." Al reeled the line in and picked up the pot. "It's your turn to find our spot and feed the team."

Violet peeked in the pot. "Can that guy feed four?"

"Not the four on our team."

They followed the river upstream, and Al was patient as Violet passed two areas she knew would be good, but this was Violet's time to shine.

"What about there?" Violet pointed to a cluster of rocks beneath the shade of an overhanging tree.

"Are you sure about that?" Al asked.

"Well, I was until you asked." Violet stepped close to the water.

"I see a few dilemmas but tell me what you're thinking." Al passed the pole to Violet. "Hold it here." She looked down. "Can you fish right-handed?"

"Yep, I can fish with both." Violet mirrored Al's hand placement, taking hold of the pole.

"Dilemma one," Al began but the powerhouse of a woman in front of her was already taking charge.

Violet flipped the line out into the river. She jigged the pole once, then twice, and got an immediate hit. She jerked the pole and stripped the line quickly, keeping perfect tension as she fought the fish's zigging and zagging maneuvers. Al stood back, her mouth open as Violet landed the fish, scooping it one-handed with the pole tucked beneath her armpit.

"Close your mouth, Alice," Violet joked as she plopped her catch into the pot.

Al incapacitated the fish and looked up to see a gorgeous smile. "You're a ringer."

Violet was so pleased with herself she could hardly respond. "I like fishing."

Al was so shocked she didn't respond to the use of her full name. "You pretended you didn't know how."

"I did not; I only said I wanted to try this time." Violet pooled the line at her feet and flipped it out beyond her rocky spot. Her hands were nimble, knowing, as she stripped the line, bouncing the tip of the pole to give extra action to the lure.

"You have to explain." Al stood close enough to avoid the pointy end of the pole as Violet cast forward off the water's top drift.

"I mentioned my aunt Eunice."

Al nodded. "You did."

"Auntie is not like most people." Violet tugged her line, flipped her wrist and cast again.

"What does that mean?" Alice asked.

"She's a bit like Stacey." Violet's eyes didn't leave the drifting line.

"You really struggle with names," Al quipped.

"I struggle with nicknames. I think it's kinda the opposite of how you feel about being called Alice."

"Really?" Al asked.

"Goes back to being called anything but Violet, but that's a whole different story."

"You've been holding out on me." Al sat on the ground near Violet's feet, captivated by the intriguing woman.

"Maybe a little." Violet chuckled. "I'm not just a silly girl who can't tie a figure-eight knot."

"That's an important knot."

"So I've been told," Violet quipped.

"And your aunt?"

"She tends to fall on the pagan side of life."

Al looked up as Violet flipped her line upstream again. "Really?"

"Yep." Violet jerked the pole, stripping her line in, and Al jumped forward to grab the wriggling trout.

"This one's nice." Al dropped it into the pot after incapacitating it.

"Enough for dinner?" Violet asked.

"This should be plenty." Al rinsed her hands in the river water as Violet reeled in their line.

"Should I break the pole down?"

Al shook her head. "You knew all along and you let me treat you like a novice?"

"If it helps, you give an excellent first lesson." Violet removed the reel and put it into the pouch before separating the pole and zipping the parts into the storage tube.

"It helps a little." There was a hint of happiness in Al's sarcastic reply. "Were you telling the truth about fileting?"

Violet nodded. "Definitely. I can do it but not well."

"Can you gut?"

Violet hated this part of hunting or fishing but it was inevitable. "I'll clean, you can cut."

They worked together at the river's edge, careful to leave as much scent at the water so that the only creature returning to camp with them would be dinner.

Violet swished her hands in the river, playing with the rocks, "Oh, look at this." She picked up a sparkly red rock, holding it in her palm for Al to see.

"It's beautiful." Al raised it to the light. "I'm not sure what it is."

"It's got to be a lucky one if it stumps you," Violet teased.

"I'm not so sure about that."

Violet shrugged. "My aunt will know. She's smart like that. Do you think the universe will mind if I keep it?"

"Generally, I'd say leave it," Alice said.

"But chicks dig red." Violet chuckled.

Alice shook her head. "Did you really just say that?"

Violet slipped the stone into her pocket. "Yep, I sure did."

Al dunked her hands into the water and rubbed them free of fishiness. "Are you ready for a fresh-caught meal?" She raised the cooking pot.

Violet tucked the pole under her arm and followed as Alice led them back to camp. "I am so very ready."

Chapter Seventeen

"Nice haul, Al." PB patted her friend's shoulder as the group celebrated the sight of a full pot. Tomorrow would be another full hiking day, and this fuel for body and soul was a definite ten.

Al waved off the accolades. "This is mostly Violet." She glanced at the smaller woman and wasn't surprised to see her satisfied, dimpled grin. "She's quite the sneaky fisherman."

"Sneaky fisherwoman," Violet clarified as she hooked the fishing gear to the backpack.

"Sorry, fisherwoman," Al repeated. She laid the filets across the pan. " I stand corrected."

"I think our Violet has quite a few tricks up her sleeve." Britt chuckled as she removed the mixed greens from PB's foraging pouch.

"I don't have many tricks, I promise." Violet sat on the ground beside the fire. "At least, not up my sleeve." She waved her hands, emphasizing the bare skin on her arms.

"Oh, I like you so damn much, Violet." PB laughed and Britt laughed too. As the joking faded, PB noticed Al staring instead of joining in. The way Al's attention landed on Violet, PB knew there were definite emotions happening between this pair.

Violet, equally observant, was intrigued by the new playfulness among the EAG team members. They were more relaxed around camp this evening. Maybe it was the change in power dynamics now that she was the solitary client, but the women felt more like friends than ever before.

"These look like a solid side dish." Al plucked at the pepper-coated, pan-fried mushrooms. "What do we have?" She raised it so PB could see.

"One of my grandmother's favorites." PB held a piece for Violet and Al to sample. "The rest of these are for the two of you. Britt and I have been eating them faster than we could cook 'em."

Violet was hesitant to take a bite. She knew the risk of mushrooms in the wild.

Al leaned in to whisper, "She's a certified forager."

Violet smiled. "Is that a real thing?" She sniffed the mushroom, smelling more of the black pepper than the earthy plant.

"A card-carrying member since I was eighteen." PB pretended to hold up an ID card. "You're safe with me."

"When she's not picking what everyone else calls weeds for herself, she's teaching people how to pick them."

"How to pick them safely," PB added. "I'll teach you, Violet. You'll never go hungry alone in the forest."

"Amazing." Violet took a bite. "This is really good."

"That's why we had to stop eating them," Britt said. "What's in the pan is about half of what we picked."

"I wish I could say it's unlike them but they tend to devour samples on the trail." Al turned the filets in the pan.

"We do have supplies for a fifth person." Britt plopped clusters of dandelion greens on their plates.

"Speaking of that." Al pushed the filets around the pan, preventing them from sticking. "We need to make decisions about the gear Greta left behind. What should stay with us and what should go."

"Most of the gear she was carrying was hers. There are some climbing ropes and day rations," PB said. "I can take up most of that."

"We can divide the food between our four packs and assume the climbing gear that way as well." Al pinched salt and pepper on the fish. "I'll carry her pack to the ranger station in the morning—"

"Why don't you let me go?" PB interrupted. "I could use a good run."

"Yeah, PB and I could hit it hard at sunrise and be back before the two of you are awake." Britt picked a few mushroom bits off of Al's plate.

Al slapped her hand. "Uh-uh, sneaky bitch," she whispered so only Britt could hear. "I thought maybe the two of you would enjoy sleeping in"—she grinned—"but mostly it's your ability to tear this camp down faster together."

"Did I suddenly become invisible?" Violet waved to get their attention. "I can help with either."

"You can stay in camp and enjoy being the client," Britt said a little more aggressively than necessary.

"Britt." Al and PB stared at the normally even-tempered guide.

"She should stay here in camp, we don't need more issues by going off script."

Al took her aside, knowing exactly what this frustration was. "There's no way we could have known."

"Snake bite—a fucking snake bite in the tent."

PB took over cooking the fish while Al and Britt walked away from camp.

"I can help cook." Violet sat beside PB.

PB used two long sticks to flip the filets over. They were almost fully cooked and she was mostly buying time so Al and Britt could settle the situation. "I appreciate that. I'm only keeping them warm at this point." She rested her elbows on her knees as she relaxed. "We have an order to things out here, a plan to take care of the team, and you—even though it is only you now—you're always going to be the priority."

"I appreciate that, but like you said, it's only me now and I'm pretty easy to boss around." Violet shrugged. She wasn't absolutely sure what she was asking for but at the very least she wanted to help.

"I'll take that into consideration, but for now you can keep enjoying the beautiful scenery."

"Oh, I am." Violet crossed her legs in front of her. "Would you mind if I asked why they call you PB?"

"I don't mind at all." PB scooped a piece of fish onto a plate and handed it to Violet.

"Are you sure I shouldn't wait for the others?"

PB raised a questioning eyebrow and Violet took the plate. "Eat."

"Thank you," Violet said. She pinched a dandelion green around a piece of fish. The joyful sound of pleasure that followed made PB smile.

"So the name thing, it kinda goes with my obsession for making jam."

"Mm-hmm," Violet mumbled as she ate.

"My grandmother was taken as a child to live in a school. They did horrible things to her, to try and make her forget her culture, but the old ways were in her blood." PB picked at the leaves on her plate. "When she came home, she made it her mission to keep tradition alive."

"What a strong woman."

PB shrugged. "I appreciate that, and the truth is she never forgot and now I will not forget either."

"And the jam?" Violet asked.

"Right. Grandmother made preserves. She experimented with everything we foraged and because I was with her, I experimented too." PB was casual as she continued. "So, Al walks into my life, or climbs, really. She's sharp as a tack, with a very similar history of building a life without the guidance of blood kin, and she sort of becomes family. Like one of those instant soups but it was definitely my grandmother's jam that hooked her in."

"That's really kind of sweet."

"Ha, funny." They shared a laugh and PB continued. "After Al fell for Grandmother's secret recipe, getting rid of her was impossible—hell, she was impossible—and my mission to enhance the recipes became an obsession for Al's taste buds."

"So why aren't you called Jam instead of PB?"

"Are you sure you aren't an investigative photographer?"

"I most definitely am not." Violet took another bite of her food and this time her satisfied moan was embarrassingly loud.

"Here's the real truth." PB moved the food closer to the coals to keep it warm. "We went on this climb—me, Al and Britt —and my grandmother sent along an amazing jar of mulberry jam. When I tell you it was good, it was better than anything you can imagine."

"Really?" Violet tried to imagine it but couldn't.

"The three of us were slathering it on those campfire biscuits along with peanut butter Britt picked up from an Amish farm stand. Anyway, this meal was literally peanut butter and jelly at the next level." PB's hands flailed, ridiculously excited as she reached the final details of the infamous nicknaming moment. "I started singing about the campfire sandwich, going on and on about how much I liked it in my belly, and Britt couldn't stop laughing. Al went with it and, just like Grandmother's jam, the nickname PB stuck."

"And you don't mind?" Violet asked, having struggled with hurtful experiences of nicknames.

"Mind? Oh, hell no. The two of them love me like no one else besides my grandmother, so it feels special."

"What's your given name?"

PB shrugged, so accustomed to the nickname that she almost never heard it said. "It's not very special."

"What's with this team and names?" Violet asked.

"I'd ask you the same thing," Al said as she and Britt returned to the campfire.

"You have a beautiful name and I'm sure that PB does, too," Violet said in a challenging tone.

"Okay, I'll tell you, but once I do you are the only one in this circle who is allowed to use it."

"I knew you liked 'PB'." Britt punched her friend's arm.

"It took a while, but from you and Al, it feels like an endless hug." PB turned to Violet. "My given name is Eustacia."

"Wait, what?" Al asked as she looked at Britt. "Have you ever heard this?"

"No, what kind of bullshit is this?" Britt was obviously surprised.

"It's Greek," PB said. "It means good grapes, or fruitful. Something like that. Grandmother always said I was the best fruit from her family tree."

"I thought it was Stacey." Al scooped fish onto her plate, smothering the greens with the roasted mushrooms.

"It is Stacey—a compromise with grandmother so I wouldn't get my ass kicked in first grade. But by the time I met you in third grade, everyone called me Stacey."

"I never knew." Britt looked up with a mischievous glint in her eyes.

"You are not allowed." PB pointed at Britt. "It's PB or nothing with you. And Violet, I officially give you permission to call me Stacey, or PB, because you've earned it."

Pretending to be offended, Britt yelled back, "How the hell did she earn it?"

PB stuffed a handful of greens in her mouth, satisfied by the moment and feeling connected to Violet in a new way. She chewed slowly, creating suspense that irritated Britt. She swallowed and giggled as she said, "She didn't really earn it. I just like her."

Chapter Eighteen

"I'm pretty sure I've underestimated you these last few days." Al lay on her back inside the tent with her legs stretched out and her ankles crossed. Free from socks and shoes, she was happy to wiggle her toes in the night air. As she tucked her hands behind her head, she stared at the seam running across the top of the tent. Al was curious about the person beside her who was anything but a fragile flower. As much as Al wanted to maintain a barrier, she knew Violet deserved better.

Violet was snuggled inside her sleeping bag with her face poking through, in what Al was calling her nightly cocoon. She wriggled her whole body to look at Al. "*You* underestimated *me*?" Violet asked. "Really?"

"You just got one of the most tight-lipped people to tell you something incredibly personal." Al rolled to her side, smiling when she saw Violet's eager face. "That's impressive."

"I like Stacey." Violet took a chance, adding, "I like you too, Alice."

"See, that's what I mean." Al chuckled. "I should want to punch you in the face for saying my name so casually." She closed her eyes as she drew a slow breath. "But all I want is to hear you say it again."

Violet clung to the sleeping bag wrapped around her. "Alice," she whispered, and watched as the lines of tension released across Alice's wrinkled brow.

"It's wild." Alice's eyes opened. "I don't think I've ever heard my name spoken aloud the way you say it."

Violet's smile disappeared inside the deep line of dimples. "I think that's a horrible injustice."

"You know what? So do I," Alice whispered, close to tears as she felt a sudden chill.

Violet felt the emotion of the moment, needing more than anything for the person in front of her to understand she recognized her courage. "I think what you did today was incredibly brave."

"Taking you fishing." Alice attempted to use humor to deflect.

"You know what I mean." Violet called out the deflection.

"It's what needs to be done." Alice rolled to her back, needing to break the spell Violet's intense eyes put her under. "You know all of those skill tests we put you through?"

"Yes," Violet said.

Alice reached to play with the string dangling from the tent's ceiling. "We do those for a reason. I've done them so much that I could tie-in to climb with my eyes closed. I can do it with gloved hands. I can even do them one-handed, because it is always about what-ifs."

Violet pulled the sleeping bag away from her face, warmed by the sincerity of Alice's tone and the intensity of her passion. "So you practice like that to react?"

Alice stared at the callouses on her hands. "We practice to act without having to think. Our muscles have memory, and sometimes every second matters."

"And the seriousness?"

"The seriousness?" Alice played.

"Don't be a bullshitter." Violet called her bluff. "You're always on edge. Doesn't it get heavy sometimes?"

Alice slapped at the dangling string, playing some kind of game as a distraction from the truth. "Sometimes it is heavy, but not always." She closed her eyes, disappearing into the memory of the morning. The screeching sound from the man in pain, the mangled bone and the blood. There had been so much blood. She opened them and looked into the brown eyes that were locked in on her, staring as though they could see her soul. "What?"

"I'd kinda like to kiss you again," Violet whispered.

"Yeah?" Alice scooted forward at the same time Violet tried to perform a repeat of her fast peck from earlier. Their foreheads knocked together with a terrible thud.

"Ow." Violet rubbed the spot.

"Ow is right." Alice mirrored Violet's reaction. "You're dangerous."

"Maybe you should stop trying to be in charge," Violet teased.

Alice rubbed her forehead. "I'm not sure I know how to do that."

Violet held up her hand, freezing the woman to the ground as she moved again into Alice's personal space. Close enough to attempt the kiss again, Violet whispered, "You'll never know until you give it a try." Her lips touched Alice's, feather light with heart-thumping tenderness. Violet returned to her place, her fingers touching her lips, cherishing every breath that followed.

Alice's eyes glistened in the darkness. It was a chaste kiss but the stoic team leader felt it from the fresh bump on her head to the tips of her naked toes. She wanted to kiss Violet again, even if it challenged every deep-rooted fear.

~~~~~~~~~~

Violet woke, aware instantly of Alice's body beside hers. She felt the rise and fall of deep sleep-induced breathing as her head rested against Alice's shoulder. The team leader lay as she had for the previous nights, uncovered and half-dressed, but Violet enjoyed the comfort of the woman's powerful body and arm holding her. She closed her eyes, feeling safe in the knowledge that in slumber there was somehow one less barrier between them.

~~~~~~~~~~

The rock wall below her was impossible to measure. Her toe curled, clenching the point of the jagged protrusion as she twisted her foot to push her hips tighter to the wall. Her toes supported the weight of her body with ease, and she trusted the belay rope would tighten to catch her if she fell.

Sliding her wrapped hand into the crevasse was the next move. It was the only move to get her closer to the sound, the echoing terror vibrating through her bones. She had to do whatever it took to reach the sound.

Her fingertips held tightly, two dagger-like talons curled over the crimp. There was a moment between momentum and release when you could not question—when you knew letting go was the only way forward. Her shoulders took the weight as her feet pushed to spring-shot her to the overhang. One hand and then the other in a perfect double dyno. There was no hesitation as every muscle in her core responded while she leveraged herself to top the slab of rock, but the force, an unknown weight against her shoulder, dragged her backward. She looked down, watching the knot on her harness slip inch by inch until it released her to fall.

Alice's heart hammered as she opened her eyes. Her gasp was loud but the weight on her shoulder prevented her from sitting upright. That weight was real as she clutched at her chest.

"What's wrong?" Violet struggled against the tangle of her sleeping bag as she moved away from Alice's body. The team leader lay half awake but completely out of sorts.

Alice closed her eyes, calming herself with three deep breaths. *It was a dream. It was only a dream.*

"Alice, are you alright?"

In the distress of the moment, hearing her name with such kindness tore the veil between her nightmare and reality. Alice placed a hand over her heart. "It was a dream," she whispered, mostly to reassure herself again, but Violet heard.

"Tell me about the dream."

Alice couldn't share, didn't want to say out loud what her sleeping mind had conjured. "It was nothing."

Violet knew it was something. "Are you sure?"

Alice nodded, realizing Violet's death grip restricted their movement. She looked down at her delicate fingers. "I'm alright."

Violet's hand fell away. "How about some water?" She passed the bottle to Alice.

"Please." Alice tugged her knees toward her chest, her heaving breaths cycling and slowing as they moved toward calm. This was not a good look for the always-reserved team leader.

Violet wondered if the way they had found themselves that morning was part of the reason for the dream. She had gotten cold in the middle of the night—she was always cold in the middle of the night, which had been a concern as she prepared to sleep in a tent with strangers. Violet was an eternal nocturnal cuddler.

"I didn't mean to get so close to you," Violet said. "I get cold when I sleep. It's a bit of a worry for me, and you're like a human space-heater."

Alice sipped her water. "You've done it every night."

The revelation embarrassed Violet. She'd hoped her cocoon-style of sleeping, which felt weird, would prevent her from inching across the tent to the obvious source of heat. "I knew it happened that first night." She covered her face. "How embarrassing."

Alice's hand reached to move Violet's, a feather-light touch followed by a whispered, "Don't be. I tend to sleep in as little as possible because I run hot when I'm at rest."

"I promise I was only trying to keep from freezing." Violet touched the water bottle. "You should drink more."

"Kinda bossy." Alice opened her mouth and guzzled what was left in the canteen. "Maybe you should be the team leader today."

"Are we climbing?" Violet asked, obviously playing along but certain she could not lead a climb.

"We'll climb tomorrow." Alice capped the canteen and rolled to find her socks. "Today is an easy hike to the next site and the four of us can set up camp. Maybe do some fishing, if daylight allows, and hopefully relax."

"So I could totally be in charge today." Violet's teasing was lighthearted. As the mood of the tent changed, their awkwardness fell away to playfulness.

"Probably, but I think PB and Britt might ask a lot of questions."

Violet's sleeping bag fell to her waist as she moved to give Alice more space. "I'm not taking either one of them on."

"I think you could hold your own." Alice tugged the shirt over her head and shimmied into her pants. "The more I get to know you…" She paused looking at the smaller woman.

"Yes?" Violet grinned.

"Well, you seem pretty scrappy to me."

"I'm mostly a lover, not so much a fighter." Violet didn't think twice about slipping off her shirt and pulling another one over her head.

"Really? Up until yesterday, I'd have thought the opposite." When Violet didn't respond, Alice explained, "You knew what to do with that hiker and with Greta"—she stared directly at Violet's mouth—"and you definitely know what to do with your lips."

Violet dismissed the mention of their mostly awkward and nearly-failed kiss as she began stuffing her sleeping bag inside the compression sack. "I have an eye for detail but not always great execution."

"You're doing fine so far." Alice placed her gear in a pile.

"If at first you don't succeed." Violet's dimpled smile appeared.

Alice snickered. "Try, try again."

"Is that an invitation?"

Alice's mouth went dry and she swallowed hard.

"Is that a yes gulp or a no gulp?"

Alice cleared her throat."I'll give you a minute to change your… you know." She pointed to Violet's sleep shorts. "I'll start a fire for coffee." Before Violet could challenge the silence, Alice disappeared behind the zipping tent door.

~~~~~~~~~~

"Peanut butter and jelly, that's what I like in my belly." PB was singing the song for the fourth time as she stirred the dehydrated fruit mixture in the pan. They'd arrived at the next site without a single mishap and as Violet and Britt set up tents, Al and PB put together a simple rehydrated high-protein meal of nuts and berries.

"It's almost always on day four."

"The two of you, I swear you're so predictable." Al opened the side pouch of her backpack. "Here." She tossed the baggie at Britt.

With fast hands, Britt snatched the bag out of the air. She didn't need to look hard to know exactly what it was. "You do love me." She pressed the back of her hand to her forehead, pretending to swoon. "I declare if you didn't love Bess so much, I might just take you as my own." She ducked as a second bag came toward her head.

Violet picked it up. "Gummy bears?" She passed the bag to Britt.

"Not just gummy bears; chocolate-covered gummy bears." Britt tore the package open and stopped to eat every last one.

"We used to joke that PB would work for a jar of jam and Britt would work for gummy bears."
~~~~~~~~~~

"*You* used to joke," PB corrected as she smeared her peanut butter and jam concoction on their biscuits. "If you had a single obnoxious vice, we'd harass you back, but…"

"Bess," Britt interrupted. "She has Bess, and I swear we can harass her about her love for that car."

"I'm not in love with Bess," Al argued.

"It's ridiculous." Britt laughed. "She pets it."

"Her," Al corrected.

"See?" Britt waved her hand. "She pets her car."

"I wash her and I wax her and sometimes I wipe her seats down because Jam Girl and her best friend Britt the Bitch can't stop eating in her."

Violet's muffled giggle turned into full laughter. "I'm so glad I listened to my gut and came on this trip."

~~~~~~~~~~

"Will it bother you if I continue reading?" Violet asked as Alice zipped the tent door.

"It's not going to bother me. It looks like you have enough light?" Alice unlaced her boots and left them by the doorway.

"Since I haven't used this at all, I have hours of light." Violet turned the book lamp on and clipped it to the ragged paperback in her hand. "I could read for at least twelve hours before changing the battery."

Alice stretched across the sleeping bag to push the cover of the book upward. The cover said *Next in Line.* "Never heard of it. Is it good?"

"Not so far." Violet tucked her finger in it to mark the page.

Al crossed her legs to get comfortable. "I guess I figured from the look of the book that it was a favorite."

Violet laughed. "Oh, no. This was a going-away present from my aunt Eunice."

"Is it her favorite?"

Violet shook her head. "I don't think she's read it at all," she said. "We do this thing where we go to a thrift store and choose random numbers to decide which book to read."

"That sounds like a terrible idea."

Violet opened the book. "Sometimes it is and sometimes it isn't, but this time it definitely was."
~~~~~~~~~~

Alice laid on her bed roll. She was yet to actually climb inside her sleeping bag or even cover her body. "Your aunt sounds pretty amazing." She kicked her feet out and flexed her toes.

"She is." Violet closed the book and stuffed it under her.

"I didn't mean to interrupt your reading."

"You didn't." Violet wrinkled her nose. "It isn't very good, anyway."

Alice turned on her side to get comfortable. "Did you enjoy the hike today?" She tucked an arm beneath her head.

Violet nodded. "It was beautiful and I think I took an entire roll of film."

"It was fun to watch you work," Alice admitted. "Since you're the only client, we'll try to give you more scenic views in the next couple of days."

"That'd be fine, but I only have two rolls left."

"I guess you're going to have to pace yourself." Alice smiled. "Take it slow."

"Are we still talking about photography?" Violet pressed her hand to the tent floor, maneuvering closer to her tent-mate.

"Wait." Alice held up a halting palm as she rolled closer. "I think, maybe…" Her voice was breathy.

"Maybe?" Violet interrupted.

"Maybe I should come to you this time." Alice's fingers danced across Violet's chin to caress her cheek. "My forehead can't handle another Violet blow." She touched her lips to Violet's. This one was not a chaste peck and Alice's lips parted to welcome Violet's tongue.

Someone moaned. Alice was sure it was her, but when Violet leaned back she looked equally satisfied.

"I think maybe I'd like to do that again." Violet waited for Alice to come back to her.

Their lips a breath apart, Alice agreed. "Once more, yes, please."

Chapter Nineteen

"Hey there, Vi. Whatcha doing?" The tone of Alice's voice was casual, as if the two of them were standing inside a bookstore browsing for their next favorite read. But they were not in the safety of a bookstore. Violet was frozen in place, clinging to the face of the rock, with Alice beside her sporting a curious smile on her face.

With the full weight of her body resting on her toes, Alice seemed to defy gravity. The same gravity Violet felt in every cell of her trembling body. "I'm—" Violet struggled to speak. Her knees were locked, her hands clenched white-knuckle tight over the crack in the stone slab.

"I can hear your breathing, and if you don't slow it down you're going to pass out," Alice said as she watched the smaller woman shift her body weight.

"I'm scared," Violet gasped.

"Put your right hand on my shoulder." Alice's voice was calm, reassuring and solid, the absolute opposite of the less experienced climber.

Violet turned her head slowly as she felt the belay rope draw up slack. "I can't let go."

Alice noticed the crack in the wall where bits of rock crumbled away and the anchoring cam had been ripped from its place. *Never trust the gear you didn't set,* Alice thought to herself as she unclipped the dangling cam. "Look at me."

Violet turned toward Alice.

"You see this?" Alice squeezed the cam two times, flexing it narrow and wide. She pounded the stone slab with the heel of her hand, checking if more rock would flake from the crack. Confident it was solid, she moved to thread the anchoring device into the opening. "Trust me, Vi. I'm placing the cam right here."

Violet listened and watched as Alice's hands moved with confidence. She didn't pause as the rope slacked just enough to secure Violet to the new anchor on the wall.

"Climber on," Al yelled. "Going down." She looked up at her team and back at Violet who was not as close to hyperventilating as she was moments before.

"I'm not sure I can let go." Violet felt a warm, strong hand curl over her own.

"You will not fall."

It was impossible to ignore the confidence in that short sentence as Alice moved her body closer. "Alice, I'm scared," Violet huffed through short breaths.

With one hand on Violet's belay rope and the other holding the wall, Alice whispered, "I will not let you fall, Violet. We are going down this wall together, just you and me on an easy climb. Lean back and walk the wall like we did an hour ago."

They'd climbed all afternoon until Violet looked up at the face of this particular rock and saw it as a personal challenge. Alice and the rest of the team took a turn, deeming it acceptable for Violet's experience level. Violet had under-cammed the crack, a novice mistake that ultimately shattered the stability of her rock wall anchor.

"Lean back, and walk down the wall Vi." Alice's jaw flexed.

"My hands won't let me." Violet's knuckles were white from their grip. Every joint that was meant to be loose and flexible in a climb was locked in a clench of survival.

Alice adjusted until her body covered the smaller woman like a human cloak. "Together. One move at a time, we go down." She looked up, trusting her life to the women belaying from the top. It was not ideal, but how could it be when Violet needed to feel safe? Alice anchored her feet and the muscles in her thighs flexed, pumped by work and adrenalin. "Put your hand on my arm," she whispered in Violet's ear. "You have to trust me."

Violet released her left hand, instantly clutching Alice's forearm with a vise-like grip.

"Violet, let the other hand go."

The voice was in Violet's ear and in her head. It was the most calming sound in the violent storm of chaos paralyzing her body. Violet released from the wall, feeling Alice against her.

"Step with me," Alice said. "Left foot."

Violet moved, silent and focused on the directions going in her ear and traveling to her feet. She stepped.

"Good. Now, right foot."

Left, right, left, right, the two bodies, joined, walked down the face of the rock wall. It felt like hours, but the entire experience was less than fifteen minutes from the moment the cam ripped from the rock until their feet touched the earth.

Violet's knees buckled when her feet hit the ground but Alice was there.

Alice's hand keyed the radio. "On the ground," she said, and the ropes slacked enough for Alice to release Violet and take hold of her.

"Sit down, Violet." Alice's hands moved over the knot on Violet's harness, freeing it so Britt or PB could pull it up.

Violet's head fell against the slab of rock behind her. She was numb, disconnected from everything but the sound of Alice's voice. She couldn't speak but she could feel, and in the moment every muscle trembled and spasmed from absolute fatigue.

"Drink some water."

A canteen was pushed in front of her face and she followed directions. Streams of liquid dribbled from both sides of her mouth, traveling down her chin to cool the heated skin of her neck and chest.

"Take a deep breath and let it out, slowly."

Violet followed the voice, listening to every word like a lost soul.

"Deep breath, again."

Violet felt her first sense of awareness as she released the second breath. Had she forgotten to breathe? What was she doing? Her eyes shot open, wide, letting in the light of the moment and what she'd experienced during the climb.

"You're doing great."

She was aware of Alice now, her hovering form tending to the panic-induced moments after the fall. "I can't believe—"

"Shh, just catch your breath and don't think about it just yet."

Violet grabbed the hand in front of her, clenching it tightly as if Alice would disappear if she let go. Alice's hands were solid but gentle in a way that reassured her she was safe. She wanted to curl into a ball and cry. She'd never been so frightened. She'd never been so close to losing all sense of time and space and she didn't like it at all.

"I don't know what I did," Violet whispered.

"You did what you had to." Alice sat beside her, hip to hip, close enough for the smaller woman to feel connected to something safe.

"The cam just gave way."

Alice pushed the canteen toward Violet's face. "Drink some more water." She wasn't worried about hydration as much as she was trying to break the thought cycle Violet was looping in. She could see that fear was smothering her.

Alice heard Britt and PB before she saw them and held up a finger to keep the silence. She stood, stepped out of her climbing gear and handed it to her team members. "We'll meet you back at camp," she whispered.

"We'll make food," PB said. They walked away without questioning Al's leadership.

Silence followed, and Alice was content to stay in it for as long as Violet needed.

Moments later, awareness hit and Violet recognized where she was and what she'd done, and asked the hard question, "I screwed it up, didn't I?"

There was no kindness in a lie, so Alice gave her honest assessment from the heat of the moment. "Nothing is predictable when we climb"—she rubbed her palms against her thighs—"but some things are true. Remember what I said the other day: we practice over and over to create muscle memory. To prevent panic."

"So I screwed up." It was a statement, no longer a question.

Alice shook her head. "*I* screwed up." She pointed at her chest.

The statement got Violet's attention and she turned fast to look at Alice. "How can it be your fault?"

"Your safety is my job, and under-camming is what caused your fall."

"I set the cam," Violet said.

"And I let you." Alice leaned forward, attempting to stand, but a delicate hand tugged her to stay.

"You taught me how to go up and how to come down but I don't think anything prepares you for falling."

Alice shrugged. "We'll work on it tomorrow."

Violet stared at her hand, still holding tight to Alice's. She felt the rough, calloused fingers wrapped with tape as she clenched tight. She didn't want to let her go.

"How are you right now?" Alice asked, feeling a sense of relief as the trembling hand found comfort in her own.

"Less freaked out, I think."

Alice looked Violet over, paying close attention to the flush returning to her cheeks. "Are you up for a hike back to camp?"

"What if I said I wasn't?" Violet's smile grew, and so did the dimples on her face.

"I guess I'd have to carry you."

Violet's eyes squeezed shut, contemplating the embarrassment, as she jumped to her feet. "There's no way I'm letting you do that."

"It gets dangerous out here after dark." Alice felt the absence of Violet's hand and pushed off the ground to stand.

"I can make the hike and I'm getting a little hungry."

"Why don't you take that off." Alice pointed to the harness around Violet's waist.

"I'll have to carry it if I do that."

Alice reached toward the buckle. "May I?"

"Yes." Violet nodded.

"Don't worry." Alice released the strap, doubled back on itself for redundant safety. "I'll take care of it."

"You're going to carry my harness, aren't you?"

Alice leaned closer to loosen the loops around Violet's thighs. It was impossible to ignore the beating of her heart and the tiny gasp escaping the smaller woman's mouth. "Part of my job is to take care of you."

"Only part of it?" Violet felt hands hover over her hips and along her thighs as Alice guided the gear down to the ground. Violet put her hands on Alice's shoulders to steady herself as she stepped out of the leg loops.

"The other part is to keep you entertained while I do it." Alice felt a rush of heat course through her body as she stood, her eyes locking on Violet's face and smile. The light reflected in her brown eyes made her pause.

"Then you've done your job today." Violet held tight to Alice. "I feel very entertained and extremely well taken care of." She tipped up onto her toes and whispered a gentle kiss on Alice's lips. "Thank you for rescuing me."

"Vi, I didn't—"

Violet pushed the stunned team leader backward, their bodies colliding as the wall of rock stopped them. "Will you just let me thank you?"

The height difference was no challenge as Alice braced herself, bending downward so Violet could take what she needed.

The meeting of their bodies was a crushing mess of fumbling passion fueled by Violet's perceived near-death experience and intensified by the release of endorphins. It was clear they wanted more than either could give at this moment. Lips smashed, tongues touched, as they needed to assure the other.

Violet pushed herself away. "Thank you." She took a deep breath, turned around and wandered down the trail toward their camp.

"You're welcome," Alice whispered to the departing woman, stunned by the tingling sensation Violet's body left behind.

Chapter Twenty

"Hey, you two, welcome back." PB set the pot of boiling water on the ground as she stepped closer to Al. Their team leader looked out of sorts as she dropped the climbing harness on the ground.

"Thanks, I think." Violet's voice trembled.

PB understood how that first fall could shake your confidence once you returned to the comfort of solid ground.

"That was a tough fall," Britt said as she set a log across the campfire. She and PB had returned to camp, built a raging fire and rehydrated a mash of high-protein stew.

It smelled like food and Violet was ready to eat just about anything they'd serve.

"Falling off is part of climbing." PB tried to lighten the mood by showing off the scar on her thigh. "Got this when I was"—she looked up, thinking, trying to remember how long ago it was.

"Fourteen." Al laughed. "And you were distracted."

"Was I?" PB touched her finger to her chin as she remembered the distraction.

"Her name was Lucy." Britt grinned as Violet caught on to the reference. "And you can pretend all you want, but that girl was no good."

Remembering the conversation with Greta, Violet confirmed, "We're all batting for the same team."

Al picked up the climbing harness and hooked it beside the others. When she turned around, she was smiling.

"I think so, if the team wants warrior princesses to show up at their next birthday party," Britt said. She raised her hand. "I want one."

"Fuck that." PB waved her off. "I want to *be* one." She stirred the pot of food a few times before scooping a portion onto Violet's plate.

"Al *is* one," Britt joked and she watched Violet's cheeks flush.

"Knock it off." Al swatted at her friend.

"Oh, come on. Look at you," Britt continued. "You could give any Amazon a run for their money." She squeezed Al's bicep. "All hard muscles."

"Uh-huh." Al took the plate from PB. "That's from catching your ass when you fall."

"As if," Britt bit back. "Maybe you're catching Jam Girl's ass but not mine."

Violet was oddly silent during the playful exchange. The friendship dynamic was something she craved but struggled to find in her everyday life.

"Like I said, falling and climbing go together like PB and Britt." Al looked up in time to dodge the flying wadded towel PB threw at her face.

Violet's voice interrupted the laughter. "It's going to happen again, I suppose." She scraped the last bite of food from her plate, more hungry than she'd realized, or perhaps lost in the monotonous action of eating.

"Hundreds of times," Britt answered.

PB added, "Thousands more if you plan to keep climbing with us."

"We climb a lot." Alice leaned closer to whisper, "Warrior princesses are always getting caught up in chaos."

Violet felt the heat rush to her cheeks but she also didn't hide her obvious curiosity as she scanned what she could see of Alice's physique.

"Hey Princess," Britt yelled. "Do we have a plan for tomorrow?"

Violet spoke before anyone else could answer. "Can we go back to the wall?" This circle of women, their confidence and unapologetic desire to challenge themselves, was empowering. She didn't want fear to stop her.

"We can," Al answered.

"I'd like to kick its ass before we try anywhere else." Violet stood, taking her plate to the tree stump they used for food preparation.

"You don't have anything to prove," PB said as she stacked her plate on top of Violet's.

Violet turned to face the rest of the team. "I have to do it for myself."

"You know, no one pointed out that Vi had a good tie-in all day," Britt shared as she added her dirty dishes to the pile.

"Not as bad with knots. That's forward progress." PB stared at Al who was taking her time with the beef mush. "Come on, slowpoke. Violet has dishes to do." She walked behind Al and picked up the towel, snapping it sharply but missing.

"I swear if that hits me, you're going down, PB."

The towel snapped again and Violet watched as the two grown women fought like childhood friends.

~~~~~~~~~~

"You've been very quiet tonight," Alice said. Like the evenings before, the team leader kicked out of her boots and freed her feet from her socks.

Violet sat crossed-legged on the sleeping bag with her book resting near the door. "I'm a little disappointed."

The evening was the coolest so far but Alice shimmied out of her pants. Her shirt came off next and she folded the clothes near her feet. Tomorrow they would wash everything and hang it out to dry. This site would be home for a few more days while Violet tackled her unanticipated fear of falling.

"Tell me what's so disappointing." Alice kicked her legs out and performed her nightly sockless toe wriggle.

"I don't like how that last climb went. How we ended the day."

"I wouldn't either." Alice turned on her side to look at Violet. "What do you want to do about it?"

"Climb more so that I'm not so afraid when it happens again."

The tent fell silent as Alice contemplated Violet's self-reflection. They'd discussed all the techniques, demonstrated what to look for and when not to place an anchoring device. The only way to get better at climbing was to climb, and Violet was about to overcome the first hurdle by getting back up on the wall.
~~~~~~~~~~

"I'll tell you what," Alice said. "Tomorrow we'll fall a little but you'll also get a chance to work on holding on when the tension of the rope isn't there."

"Free climb?" Violet asked.

"No, we aren't there yet, but if you really want to climb, I can see free climbing as part of your future." Alice tipped her chin to point at the abandoned book. "How's the story?"

Violet chuckled. "There was a reason that book was at a thrift store."

"That bad?"

"So much worse," she replied. "With a title like *Next in Line*, I should have left it there and picked whatever *was* the next in line."

"That's terrible."

"At least it's a paperback." Violet chuckled. "We could always use it in an emergency."

"For an ass emergency?" Alice joked.

"Ahh, no. Ew." Violet shook off the gross images in her head. "I was thinking maybe for starting a fire."

"That's useful, too, although you've got great skills when it comes to that."

'Thank you." Violet pulled off her shorts and slid inside her sleeping bag. "And if I was going to pick a book to wipe my ass with, it would definitely be *Next in Line*."

Alice laughed. "I'll take it off my to-be-read pile." She laid across her bed roll and wriggled to get more comfortable. They were silent for a while, listening to the wind ripple the material of the tent.

Violet's head filled with thoughts of the woman beside her, about the person her team leader truly was. Alice was serious, but only to build confidence. She was powerful, yet extremely attentive and gentle. Violet felt these conflicting characteristics were exactly the combination she needed right now. Timing was everything.

"Alice?" she whispered.

"Yes." Alice rolled to her side to answer.

"Would you kiss me goodnight?" Violet asked, and before words were spoken or doubts could interfere, the taller woman scooted to fill the space between them.

"I was kinda hoping you'd ask."

Violet leaned close enough for a kiss and a strong arm came around her hip, rotating the two until she was resting atop Alice, her leg slipping to rest between the other's.

Violet pressed her palms beside Alice's head, pivoting to arch up and simultaneously grinding their hips together. "A kiss." She forced the words as she kissed Alice.

"Is that all you want?" Alice asked.

Attempting to catch her breath, Violet tried to duck her head but slammed Alice hard in the nose.

"Oh, fuck." Alice bucked forward, rolling Violet to the side as she clutched her face. "Oh, for fuck's sake." She pulled her hand away.

"You're bleeding." Violet sat up. "Oh, jeez, I broke your nose."

"You didn't break it. You just popped it."

"What can I do?" Violet scrambled to find a piece of material to dab the bleeding.

"Well, for one, you could let *me* kiss *you* like you asked." Alice chuckled as Violet tried to move away. "I'm fine, Vi." She grasped the small, trembling hands. "Look at me."

"I'm a terrible mess." Violet closed her eyes.

"Look at me, Violet." Alice squeezed Violet's fingers until the woman looked at her. "You're beautiful and wonderful and all I want to do is kiss you without bleeding or needing an ice pack after."

Violet laughed. "We don't have any ice packs."

"Then come here." Alice tugged her hand. "Sit with me and let's try it again."

~~~~~~~~~~

Vi woke in the same position as the night before but this time she knew she was welcome to stay. She felt a cramp but didn't want to wake the woman sleeping beside her. If she rolled on her back to stretch the muscle in her thigh, she'd wake Alice. Her body tensed as she gripped the drawstring around the face of her sleeping bag. She rolled sideways but met with resistance.

"Are you okay?" Alice whispered.

Violet shook her head. "I have a cramp in my thigh."

"Can I help?"
~~~~~~~~~~

Violet chuckled. "You just want to get inside my sleeping bag." The shudder was either from laughter or excitement, Violet couldn't tell, as Alice rolled to straddle her.

"Can I unzip and take a look?"

Violet nodded. The sleeping bag zipper pulled down and she felt the rush of cold night air against her skin, and the muscle cramped tighter.

"The cold isn't helping," Violet whispered.

Alice rubbed her hands together, hoping the friction would warm them as she slid her palms up Violet's leg. "Where does it hurt?"

Her question was serious but Violet struggled to answer. Alice didn't have soft hands but they were definitely strong when she found the hardened muscle on the back of Violet's thigh.

Violet gasped. "Yep, you found it." She wanted to change position, shift away from the massage, because the spot she was feeling it most wasn't anywhere near where Alice was.

"Getting better?" Alice asked seriously.

"Alice, if it gets any better I might have an orgasm."

Alice's hands stopped moving. "Violet."

"Please don't stop," Violet pleaded. "I want you and I know you want me too."

"We can't do this here." Alice pulled her hands away. "My best friends are sleeping ten feet away."

Violet grabbed Alice's hand so the woman would lay beside her. "Kinda kills the mood, I guess."

"Yeah, it really kinda does."

~~~~~~~~~~

"You did it!" Britt held a hand up for Violet to slap with a high five.

They were standing atop the huge rock wall that had defeated Violet the day before. PB was at the ready, belaying Al as she reached the top a few seconds behind. It was a personal triumph that all of them were celebrating, with Violet wearing the biggest smile.

"I did it." She tugged the rope on her harness. "I got to that hold and tugged the cam a few times to be sure and I did it."
~~~~~~~~~~

"You sure as hell did." Britt cheered as Violet's enthusiastic arms wrapped around her tightly.

PB was next in line. "Calm down, tiger. You'll hug us off this ledge."

"Oh, sorry. I'm just so happy."

"You should be." Al put an arm over PB's shoulder to join the hug. "You did everything right today."

Violet looked up into Alice's smiling face, noticing the bruise on the team leader's nose, remembering what led to that mark and how important Alice was to one of the best weeks of her life.

Al was nearly tackled by Violet's hug. "It was amazing to watch you climb," she said as her arms fell away. Al felt the stare from her best friends. PB and Britt were obviously curious about Violet's lingering hold on the team leader.

Britt began wrapping the climbing rope pooled at her feet. "Are we going to climb again or hike back to camp?"

PB waited for the answer as Violet lingered close to Al.

"How do you feel?" Al's voice was choppy, far from the level of self-control she normally had.

"I feel like I could do that all day."

"Climbing euphoria is a sneaky bitch," PB said. "That means we better get her back to camp."

"Seriously?" Violet questioned.

"Don't worry." Al leaned close. "We've got more climbing ahead of us."

~~~~~~~~~~

They had plenty more climbing days and even more chilly nights. One night, Violet was feeling a level of confidence that made her feel bold.

"How would you feel about starting the night together?" Violet asked as she wriggled into her sleeping bag.

"You mean together, together? So you can skip the cold-temperature scoot you're going to do at midnight?" Alice joked. She was stretched out like she had every night of the trip, her toes wriggling in the cool air, free from the confines of socks and boots.

"If you don't mind me stealing all of your body heat, I'd kinda like to scoot," Violet confessed.
~~~~~~~~~~

Alice raised her arm, inviting Violet to sleep with her. It was comforting, the way the smaller woman tucked against her. The fit was right.

"Are you sure I won't make you too hot?" Violet's question, asked innocently, sounded more suggestive after leaving her mouth.

Alice's body shook as she chuckled. "I'm always hot, remember?"

"Hot-ter?" The nuanced delivery was not accidental.

Alice's arm tightened around Violet. "You most definitely make me hotter, but don't worry. I can handle all the heat."

Chapter Twenty-One

"How did that climb feel?" Britt asked.

"Today felt so good." Violet's response was animated as she waved her hands and trekking poles. She was walking behind Britt who was her solitary guide that afternoon. PB and Alice had left camp a few hours earlier to hike ahead, focused on scouting an off-trail climbing location. As they hiked, Violet missed having Alice behind her.

"That first set of boulders weren't a big deal, but the way Stacey demonstrated falling off and holding on after, it all clicked together for me."

"I could tell," Britt said. "The confidence shows."

Britt's kind words and honest observations were the boost Violet needed. After her panic fall days earlier, and the triumphant second attempt, she'd wanted to continue to challenge herself. "I like that we didn't have to fight other hikers for climbing time."

"It helps that we're so remote."

For the last five days they'd hiked deeper into the forest to climb in locations less traveled. Al and PB studied maps and routes put together by fellow climbing teams. Today would be Violet's biggest challenge and also the most isolated.

"It feels like the outside world doesn't exist." Violet stuck her trekking pole into the dirt.

"If you haven't noticed, this is where EAG is at our very best." Britt chuckled. "We tend to be outside the limits of technology."

"It's fun."

"It's also simpler." Britt stopped to check the compass hanging from her backpack's shoulder strap. "Come this way," She pointed toward the hip-high grassy field. It wasn't a worn trail, matted down like the one they were on. Instead, it was a narrow separation of tall wildflowers and plants; a path obviously made for the rest of the team by PB and Alice.

"Britt, was this the original plan?" Violet asked. She released her trekking pole to let the grass brush against her fingertips.

"What do you mean?"

"Are we out here off trail because it's only me?"

Britt stopped. "Mostly, yes. Al thought you'd like this part of the forest and PB and I wanted to teach you in areas that aren't crowded by tourists and novice climbers."

"I guess I should feel guilty, but I don't."

Britt led Violet to the edge of a river. "Don't feel guilty. Life is unpredictable and sometimes this is how it happens. Enjoy the exclusive treatment."

Violet watched the water ripple over the rocks. "Can I?" She patted the camera on her hip.

"Sure, we're waiting here for Al anyway."

Violet dropped her backpack and poles on a large boulder and set herself up to fill her camera's film with everything her eyes could take in. The sunlight shimmered on the water, and Violet crouched to her knees to capture the moment.

Through the unfocused lens, she saw a figure step from the tree line. Her body felt the presence. At full height, in all her gear, Alice looked like a catwalk supermodel—if they were covered in dirt, and wet with sweat. Violet adjusted the focus on her lens, zooming out to take the picture. She clicked once, advanced the film, readjusted to focus on the smirking half-grin, and shot again. Alice was stunning.

"Hello over there." Alice waved.

"Hey, guys." Britt checked her watch. "You're right on time."

"Are you ready to cross yet?" Alice squatted down to get her attention, unaware that she was the focus of Violet's viewfinder.

Violet snapped another picture. "I think so. The water looks fast."

"The water is always fast," Alice joked.

Britt interrupted, "Unless it's not."

"We'll take it slow," Alice reassured Violet, locking arms with PB who had anchored herself to a tree with ropes and a harness. "Coming to you," she yelled and tossed the rope to Britt. The rigging of rope might have been excessive, but a single misstep could send any one of them downstream. With their rope pulled over the narrow stretch of the river, they could cross without wasting energy that could affect the rest of their day.

Alice met Violet at the opposite side of the water. "We've got a super climb all set up." She held a hand out to Violet. "Hands on the rope and on me." She hooked an arm through Violet's bent elbow.

"Should I be this excited?" Violet's smile was wide, her dimples like joyful craters as the cold water rushed against her shins.

"Yes, you should." Alice placed her body so Violet was sandwiched between the rope and herself. Adrenaline-rush moments like this were the reason she put EAG together.

The crossing was simple, mostly because the water level never reached above their knees. It was cold and refreshing, and once they were safe on shore, PB led the team to their new campsite.

"This is cozy." Britt laughed. "Did you make a broom?" The site looked to be swept of debris.

"We had to build a ring and set up the tents," PB said. "Not much of a challenge." She looked at her watch. "We've been roasting marshmallows for hours waiting on you two."

"Violet had rolls of film to shoot," Britt joked.

"Roll, I had a roll, and there are seven pictures left." Violet was unlacing her boots so she could set them in the sun to dry.

Alice already had her boots off and was wiggling her toes near the heat of the coals as PB fed a few small pieces of wood onto the smoldering embers.

"That river crossing was fun." Violet said. "Is that the only time we'll do one?"

"The plan is to hike out the last two days. We aren't going to backtrack but we'll definitely get wet again," Alice explained.

"I can't believe this is my life right now." Violet rested against her backpack. "I'm so happy I came on this trip."

"I think you're almost part of the team." Britt placed her boots beside Violet's.

"Your climbing has definitely improved," PB added.

"We talked about that earlier," Britt said. "I think our Violet is having some feelings about being the only client."

Alice sat beside Violet. "The best feelings to have are the ones that put that smile on your face."

"Yeah?" Violet leaned closer.

"Absolutely."

Britt looked at PB and PB shrugged. It was impossible to miss the change in behavior of their team leader. Al was definitely gentler and less edgy when it came to Violet. Perhaps it was Violet's panic during the climb a few days ago that softened Al. Whatever it was, PB and Britt liked the easy way the current excursion was shaping up.

"Who's hungry?" PB asked.

Three hands shot up. "Me."

"I've put together a stunning bucket of greens and Al was kind enough to stir up some stew."

"I rehydrated it with care," Al joked and the rest of the team played along.

~~~~~~~~~~

"I can't believe I was so hungry," Violet said as she dunked the plates in the river.

"We've been out here for a week. Working hard every day, it'll change you," Alice was knee deep in the river collecting water for them to boil while PB took Britt to the climbing location.

Violet and Alice were alone for the first time in days and Violet had plans for her team leader. "A lot about me has changed." She waited for Alice's reaction to her statement.

Holding the water bladder, Alice stilled as her attention moved to Violet. "Yes, this trip wasn't what I expected." She capped the container and carried it to shore.

Violet set her plates on the rock, her voice breathy as she asked, "What did you expect?"

Alice shook the water from her hand before tucking a stray hair away from Violet's cheek. "I definitely wasn't expecting you."

Violet tipped up on her toes. "No?" she teased.

Alice lifted the smaller woman, bringing her close. "Oh no. You are quite the surprise."

"You surprised me too." Violet hooked her finger in the collar of Alice's shirt. "How's your nose?" She began her survey.

"Nose is fine."

"And your forehead?" Violet caressed the spot.

"Forehead's good."
~~~~~~~~~~

"And your hand?" Violet kissed her palm.

"My hand is—"

"Good?"

Alice nodded. "We have to stop meeting that way," she teased.

"There are other ways, you know." Violet held onto Alice as a gentle touch of her lips drew their bodies closer together.

Alice lifted Violet, stepping once and twice until they met the wall of rock along the shoreline.

Violet's feet touched the ground and she took that moment to spin a stunned Alice and pin her to the rock. Violet's heart raced, her blood pumping to awake erotic places. "Do you realize we are finally alone?"

"Mm-hmm." Alice swallowed hard.

"And that I've had to keep my hands to myself for days." Alice chuckled. "And nights."

"Oh, the nights are the hardest." Violet pressed Alice's back tighter to the wall as she kissed her. "Your hot body wrapped around mine."

"This might not be the most—" Alice's voice caught when Violet's lips found the hollow of her throat and moved to the newly exposed skin on her chest.

"This might be," Violet whispered against pebbling skin, a smile forming as she took pleasure in Alice's reaction.

"Violet." Alice's hands fell, surrendering to the explorations as she felt the snaps on her shirt pop one by one.

"Why so many clothes?" Violet opened the shirt and dragged the tucked T-shirt from the waist of her pants.

"I don't want to get cold," Alice panted, unsure if the days of wanting were finally coming to an end.

"Have you ever been cold?" Violet joked as she pushed her sports bra up, exposing the dark circle surrounding her nipple.

"I don't know what—" Alice lost her ability to form words as Violet's lips covered her breast. Violet had every intention of devouring Alice in this untamed place. The sound of zipper teeth ticking and the hand slipping against her abdomen rocked Alice to the core. "Vi," she rasped.

"Can I touch you, Alice?"

Alice's mouth ran dry as she arched into the icy fingertips. "Please. Yes, please."

Those words, the absolute surrender, shattered any reservation as Violet's fingers touched the warm flesh above Alice's sex. Everything behind the intense rigid exterior Alice presented, all of it, disappeared with a single touch.

"Oh, Alice." She felt the want against her fingertips as she moved to touch warm folds. At that moment, Violet needed to know all of her. She entered with one slow finger, dancing the others around her sex. Alice gasped and that was all the coaching Violet needed, making her hungry for more. "You like that." It wasn't a question as Alice's whole body arched into Violet's.

"Yes," Alice choked out. "I love it. I want it," she said as her palms slapped against the rock slab beside her.

Violet slipped her finger out, plunging slowly again with two fingers deep inside. She wanted this woman more than she thought possible and all apprehension left as she felt Alice move with her. She followed the rhythm of Alice's hips, over and again, drawing tiny figure eights as she brushed her clit. She was close, Violet knew as she felt the clench of tight abs against the heel of her wrist, and the slick warmth covering her hand. Violet celebrated the obviously euphoric moment internally as Alice trembled against her.

Alice's breath hitched, her hand coming around to draw Violet against her. She was reaching, clutching, grasping for a climax she wanted more than ever. Violet paused long enough to tease.

"Vi," Alice begged the smaller woman until her body arched, tensing through her core into the climax.

Violet wanted to stay in this moment forever. Her hand stilled, cupping warm flesh with no intention to withdraw. Her forehead fell against Alice's shoulder, needing to regain a sense of where they were and how to have her again. She raised her chin and Alice's eyes opened. The hunger in her stare was impossible to miss.

"Violet," Alice said, barely recognizing her breathy voice, "I want to have you." She tugged at the shirt tucked into Violet's hiking shorts. Their bodies separated to allow Alice's shaking hands to unfasten Violet's button.

It was fitting that their passionate dance played against the sun-warmed rock wall beside a raging river. The sounds of nature and her own beating heart were almost hypnotic as Alice spun the woman to switch their positions. She hesitated as Vi wriggled her hips, releasing her clothes to the ground.

"Oh," she groaned as talented fingers slid into her low-cut briefs.

"Violet," she whispered, asking and answering a thousand questions with a single touch.

"Alice," Violet gasped. Her hands cupping Alice's face.

The pause was abrupt. "Vi?" Alice questioned.

With desperate, breathless gasps, Violet explained, "Oh yes, I want you to, but I've never done it like this. I'm not sure I can if I'm standing."

Alice dropped to her knees, tugging down the last barrier between herself and Violet's body. She looked up into wanting eyes. "It's not that you can't come standing up." Alice grinned as her thumbs caressed up the length of bare thigh, parting Violet's legs until she could place one over her shoulder. "It's just that you haven't." She kissed the soft flesh of Violet's sex, whispering with a slow touch of tongue, inch by inch. With a feather-soft press of lips, her mouth took the woman in front of her. Alice felt the weight of Violet's body as she unwound against her lips. This woman was paradise. An oasis Alice never wanted to leave and she worshiped over and over again.

It was impossible to hide the moment of climax when Violet's hips jerked and Alice felt the clench of hands in the loose tangles of her hair. She looked up, feeling more emotion than she could read in the naked body above hers. Violet was more than she ever thought possible and yet it was still not enough.

She lowered Violet's leg, careful not to let go of the woman pressed against the wall of rock.

"I don't want to move," Violet rasped a chuckled confession.

Alice pressed her body close. "I don't want to either."

Exhausted, Violet's arms draped around Alice's hips and with an extraordinary amount of effort, she kissed Alice's bare chest. "That was pretty wonderful," Violet whispered.

"Yeah." Alice's forehead touched Vi's. She wanted more.

Violet couldn't feel her legs or her hips or any other part besides the pounding of her heart and the offset rhythm of Alice's. She felt a trembling hand cup her cheek. "Oh, yeah."

Alice could see the truth in those two words. "Violet, I don't know what to say."

Violet's face relaxed against the strong hand. "All you have to say is that this isn't the last time, that it's the first of many more."

"It is. It's all of that." Alice's lips touched Violet's before she drew their bodies together.

"That's what I need, Alice." Violet paused.

"Alice, yes. Please only ever call me Alice forever."

Chapter Twenty-Two

"I can't sleep," Violet whispered.

"I know." Alice chuckled as she held tightly to Violet.

Violet relaxed against Alice. "I'm sorry. I can't stop thinking about how you make me feel." She rolled over to look at Alice, wanting to read her expressions as they talked.

"And what is that?" Alice asked.

"Everything," Violet whispered. "You make me feel all of the things and it's not what I was planning."

"I wasn't planning it either." Alice pressed her lips to Violet's forehead.

"You're really beautiful," Vi said. "Not just on the outside, and I'm pretty sure you don't share the inside very much."

"No, not very much."

"I love the way you touched me," Violet said. "I want you to do it again."

"I want to do it again, too." Alice smiled. "If it helps."

"It helps. It helps a lot."

~~~~~~~~~~

"How does it feel?" Alice asked as she caressed the tape wrap around Violet's hand.

"Loose but tight"—Violet's dimples appeared—"if that makes sense."

"That makes perfect sense. We want to create a barrier so you can wedge your hands, but we also want full circulation."

Violet opened and closed her hands. "It feels right."

Alice's fingers clenched Violet's as their eyes met. The silent conversation was more than client to team leader, and Violet was touched by the vulnerability of the gesture.
~~~~~~~~~~

"You're up, Britt." Alice sidestepped so her team could take charge.

"I want you to tie in," Britt said as she stood beside Violet, knowing she was about to attempt the most challenging climb of the week.

Violet would place her anchoring cams and work the cracks and holds to top the twenty foot slab of stone. For anyone with experience, it would take less than twenty minutes and ropes would slow them down, but for Violet this would be a mind over matter pinnacle climb.

"A figure eight, just like I taught you," Britt encouraged.

Violet stretched her arm out to the side and twisted a loop where it bent, to make the first part of the knot. She looked at Britt. "Is it right so far?"

Britt nodded.

PB began her own tie in. "You're doing great, Violet."

It was like having her own private cheer squad on a sideline as the experienced members built Violet up to tackle this challenge.

"Preventing an overlap is the tricky part." Britt's hands moved at Violet's pace, waiting for each twist and loop to weave into a perfect figure eight anchored to the harness around Violet's hips and thighs.

"Hell yeah," Violet said as she cinched the knot tighter. Her confidence was at an all-time high, matching the adrenaline rush as she heard the official readiness call.

"Climbers on," PB said to the belaying team.

Violet repeated, "Climbers on."

Britt's hands moved over the ropes on PB's harness as Al checked and double-checked Violet's.

"You've got this," Alice whispered, wanting more than anything to kiss her for good luck.

There was safety in redundancy as they tied their belay devices in and performed an additional check. The setup for the morning's climb was Violet and PB on the wall, and Alice and Britt the belayers on the ground.

"Climb," Al and Britt said.

It was going to be a side-by-side ascent. Britt would move at Violet's pace, observing until there was hesitation or fear preventing Violet from proceeding. Violet attacked the challenge without hesitation.

She gripped the lip of the stone with the toe of her shoe. She could see the next hand-hold but with her limited height she would have to use the power in her thighs to rotate against the face of the rock. She paused, reaching for a bit of chalk to dry her sweating fingers.

"Take your time, Violet," she whispered to herself as her fingertips hooked into a hold. It felt tight, perfectly solid as her foot pivoted and she leveraged higher. She was reading this wall, hold for hold.

"She's a completely different climber," Britt said as she took up slack on PB's rope.

"She's definitely different."

Violet looked up and back down at the belaying team. She was halfway and it felt incredible. She'd never been more confident.

"You're a natural, Vi." PB felt the tug on her rope, and knew without question the cinch was too tight. She looked down to yell at Britt, "Hey, let up some slack."

PB saw the reason for Britt's anchoring pull, giving her and Violet nowhere to go but up. A big cat was hunting them in a predatory position—scrunched on its haunches, pivoting side to side, ready to pounce. "Holy fuck."

Violet's eyes followed PB's to the team below. Al and Britt were in the path of a hungry cougar, and from their elevated position there was nothing she or PB could do.

"Find a good hold," PB said as an eerie silence fell between them.

"Fuck, Al!" Britt cinched the belay rope tighter. She was first in line, and would take on the animal before either climber could descend.

"Can you pull your knife?" Al asked in a voice too calm for the situation. She wanted to release her rope. She knew PB could grab hold and come down on her own, but Violet wouldn't know what to do.

Britt locked the belay device in one hand, and with the slowest motion possible she tried to draw the knife from her hip. It was a straight blade—the only one available to either of them on the ground. Her feet slid through the dirt, moving with the knowledge that it wasn't slow enough to prevent an attack.

The cougar watched every movement, as if each slide of Britt's foot tugged the bowstring of its attack tighter.

"What do we do?" Violet asked. She felt safe where she was, but trapped at the same time. Should she go up or go down and face whatever was going to happen?

"Al is about to let go of my rope and I'm pretty sure Britt isn't going to have a choice." PB moved horizontally to tie herself to Violet. "You and I are going to move down. Not all the way but close enough so that when the ropes release our falls will be shorter."

A scream echoed around them, and Violet didn't hear any of PB's words. The huge cat was on Britt, gnawing at her defending hand as she tried to fight with the other. Blood sprayed, but Violet couldn't tell where it was coming from. PB's rope released and she clipped into Violet's harness. Everything happened fast as Al's line slacked, relying on PB to cover Violet. No longer on the belay line, Al threw herself between Britt and the raging animal.

In shock, Violet released her hand, and the length of her safety line tied to PB went tight, leaving her tethered fifteen feet from the ground. She could fall from that height with minor injuries, she hoped. Her first thought was getting to the team below.

Another scream sounded, spiraling up to PB and Violet as Al plunged Britt's knife over and over into the giant cat's neck. The animal seemed possessed, thirsty for the taste of blood coming from Britt's fighting hand.

Violet was trapped on the end of her rope with nowhere to go while the belayers fought on the ground. PB anchored Violet to the rock face. Moved like a spider and pushed off the wall ten feet from the rocky surface below. She collapsed when her feet hit and scrambled to stand, and Violet watched in horror as the three team members fought the attacking animal.

Violet gasped when Alice fell against the big cat, toppling onto Britt. PB's leg was malformed like the hiker's arm earlier in their excursion. Her foot was twisted in an opposing direction of its natural position.

Violet took a chance and pulled slack on her rope. It released enough for her to move closer to the ground. She'd never felt more useless in all her life as the heap of climbers lay in a pool of blood below her. She clutched the hand holds she'd used on her ascent, following the chalk-marked path. She gripped, pulled slack and moved down. She repeated this a few more times until she felt confident her feet would land on the ground. When she released, she pulled slack enough to untie.

PB lay clutching her fractured leg, her back to the rock. "Help them first," she grunted.

Violet reached for Alice, touching her throat for a pulse. It was pounding hard enough to see before she felt it.

"I'm afraid to let the cat go." Alice's right hand held a knife handle, the blade buried deep in the animal's neck. Blood poured from the abundant wounds, making it impossible to know who in the pile was bleeding.

Violet could see the lifelessness in the animal's glassy eyes. "I'm pretty sure it's dead."

Alice yanked her hand, drawing the blade out of the animal. She rolled to her side, immediately aware that Britt was trapped underneath. There was no hesitation as Alice dropped the knife and tore the big cat off her friend. The animal must have weighed as much as Violet, but Alice tossed it like it was nothing. She had one goal and it was to save the woman bleeding on the ground.

"First aid, Violet," Alice yelled, and the smaller woman raced to the backpack on the ground. What could they possibly do with the limited supplies inside the little red bag?

Violet unzipped the pouch. "What do you want?"

"We have to stop the bleeding."

Britt's body torqued as she clutched her bloody hand. Violet saw that two fingers were missing. There was nothing they could do to save them, even if she had time to look for them. They had to focus on what was left.

"Al, fuck. It hurts so much." Britt curled into a fetal position.

"I know, Britt." Al rolled her onto her back, finally able to assess the damage. Her best friend was ripped across her torso and sliced through her arm, and blood dripped from her shredded hand. "This is gonna hurt." She pulled her shirt over her head. "Give me the knife," she said to Violet, and the smaller woman was there, passing everything Alice asked for without hesitation.

"Cut my shirt open." Alice felt for the water bottle on the side of the backpack. She poured the entire contents on Britt's hand. The wound was devastating but she needed to save what was left. "There's a flat roll of reinforced tape. Find it."

They went back and forth like a surgical team, until Britt was bandaged enough to move. Al turned to PB, suddenly aware that her second team member had broken her leg. "Fuck!" she yelled. "Where's your radio?" she asked PB.

"Under the—" PB's head tipped toward the cougar.

"Vi, do you think you can help PB?"

Violet nodded.

Al kicked at the cat and rolled it over to find the small bag PB usually had clipped to her waist. The radio wasn't there. "You sure?" she asked, relying most on the adrenaline pumping through her body.

"I don't know. I'm not sure of anything." PB winced as Violet bent to help her stand.

"It's fine." Al folded the first-aid kit and jammed it into the backpack. She threw the bag on her shoulder and stumbled to Britt's side. "How much can you move?"

Britt couldn't answer. Her eyes glazed and her body fell limp.

"She's going into shock," Violet yelled.

Al took off her backpack. "Come here." She waved Violet close.

Violet steadied PB against the wall of rock and, before she could ask, Alice whipped her around, threw the backpack over her shoulders, anchored it to her chest and spun her back to PB. "We're going. You're on PB, I've got Britt."

Britt screamed as Alice tied her bloody hand tightly to her chest. There was no way to keep it elevated, and she wanted as much pressure as possible to slow the bleeding. Britt passed out from the pain, doubling her weight.

"Go!" Al yelled at Violet and PB. "We're right behind." Al shouldered Britt with her best fireman's carry and stomped to her feet. It was a mile to camp, and right now that was her only goal.

Chapter Twenty-Three

"Can I help you?" Violet asked as she lowered PB to the ground. The group had made it back to camp a weary and bloodied mess.

"It's only broken. No blood or anything." PB waved Violet away. "Go help Al."

For a moment, PB was the least of their worries as Violet watched Alice stumble into camp with an unconscious Britt draped over her shoulder. Alice did her best to lower the woman gently but the thud made all of them wince. Britt only grunted, which wasn't a good sign.

"We need to put out the fire. And I need to radio for help." Alice was all go and no pause as she dropped their bags to the ground.

"I've got the fire," Violet said. There were a few pieces of smoldering wood but most of their gear was packed for their hike to the next camp. They were the farthest from civilization they'd been in twelve days and Violet was scared, admittedly.

"Al," PB groaned against the pain and frustration, struggling to help. "Britt's pack has the SAT phone."

That was all she needed to hear. Al was on her knees, digging through the outer pocket. "If you can talk, you can call." She handed the palm-sized device to PB.

"Got it," PB nodded, then yelled at Violet, "We're going to have to move faster. I need you to help me stabilize this break." She patted her knee just above the contorted fracture. The lines on her forehead were deep, and her breath ragged, as she prepared to have the damage splinted.

"I've got you," Violet whispered. With a quick explanation from PB of what to do, the painful work of immobilizing began. "This is going to hurt," Violet said apologetically.

PB grabbed a stick from the ground. Through gritted teeth, she said, "Just do it." She bit down on the stick.

Violet secured PB's break, and the two of them turned when they heard Britt scream.

"Fuck," Al yelled as she checked the wrap securing the bloody arm to Britt's chest. It was soaked through. Her hands traveled Britt's body, and one after the other she found multiple punctures—deep bleeding bite marks left behind from the attack. Al felt her own hip and saw her wound, but moved her focus back to Britt.

The first-aid kit was open on the ground but there wasn't much left. Violet knelt beside Alice. "PB is ready to move. How can I help you?"

Alice stared at Violet. "I can't get the bleeding to stop, and she can't stay awake long enough to keep pressure on it. If I put on a tourniquet, it might kill her hand or whatever is left of it. I have to stop the bleeding. That's what..."

Violet passed the velcro strap to Alice. "We've got a long hike. It's the only thing we can do."

The nonverbal understanding that passed between them was eerie. Alice was covered in blood, and Violet worried that some of it belonged to the team leader who hadn't taken the time to let Violet check.

Alice tore at the shredded shirt so she could lock the tourniquet in place, cinching just enough to slow the bleeding. Britt's thumb was gone and her index finger dangled by tendon and bone. "I need another shirt to rewrap this. Hopefully we won't attract another hungry cat on the way out of here."

Alice had only her sports bra and shorts on. In a few hours, the sun would go down, and she'd need more protection as they raced to exit the park.

Violet dug through the backpack. "Put this on, Alice." She set the shirt in front of the woman, but Alice reached into her pocket and realized her knife was gone. "Damn it." She swore as she bit down on the hem of the shirt and ripped it in strips for a bandage.

Violet watched as the team leader did what she was best at... being calm in a storm.

"There's another roll of reinforced tape in the mess kit," Alice said as she began to bundle Britt's hand.

Violet was there seconds later and she watched Alice rotate the tape round and round the makeshift bandage until Britt's hand looked like a defensive weapon and not a bloody wound.

Al turned her attention to PB. "Tell me what you need." She surveyed the trekking poles tied tightly to her friend's leg. It was enough to get her out. "Can you move like that?"

"With Violet's help, yeah." PB winced as she attempted to stand. "You're bleeding, Al."

"It's fine." Al pressed her palm against the waist of her shorts and it came away bloody. "It's a scrape."

"Violet, check her before we move."

Alice's eyes were questioning as Violet stepped close enough to the team leader. "I'm going to unzip your shorts." Violet knelt in front of her but knew before she touched Alice that it was more than a scratch. The fabric was ripped through, shredded by claws and teeth—she couldn't determine which—and the blood coming from her hip was more than a trickle.

Violet pulled the shorts down enough to see the tear in Alice's hip. She'd left gentle kisses on that hip only days before. Alice's beautiful body had become a barricade between the members of her team and the animal's attack. "This is not a scratch," Violet said.

There were deep sets of punctures surrounded by terrible tears of flesh. It was obvious that Alice had used her own body to save her best friend's life.

"I'm fine." Alice tugged at her pants.

"We need to stop the bleeding or you'll never be able to carry her out." Violet's voice was shaky yet commanding, but Alice couldn't think about herself when Britt lay bleeding.

"The bottle of alcohol in the kit. Grab that," PB yelled.

Violet found the sealed container. She looked into Alice's eyes, attempting to distract her as she poured. "This is going to hurt."

Alice braced herself on Violet's shoulder's and clenched her teeth as the liquid ran through the open wound, washing the blood away. "I'm going to bandage it." Violet used another shirt to cover the wound and tied a hard knot over the top. She had to hope the improvised bandage created enough pressure when she fixed Alice's shorts back in place. "Is that too tight?"

"I can't even feel it." Alice was finished being still. She had no time or patience. They needed to move. "Is the fire out?"

"It is." Violet steadied herself to stand, and Alice held out a hand to help her.

"Are you hurt?" Alice asked, and Violet stopped to check herself for the first time.

"Bumps and scratches"—Violet held out her hands—"but that's nothing new for me."

"Are you strong enough to help PB?"

Violet nodded. "I am, and you'll be able to focus on Britt."

"Let's go." Al removed everything from her backpack that would slow them down. "First-aid kit and water." She handed it to PB. "Can you carry this?"

"I can." Violet slipped it over her shoulders and locked it in place across her chest. There was no question this was how it had to be.

"I want the two of you in front," Alice ordered as she slipped the climbing rope over her head to rest on her shoulder. "Watch for snakes and don't stop unless you have to."

"What about you?" Violet asked.

"I'll be right behind you." Alice knelt in front of Britt. "Hey." The word was a warning. "I've got to pick you up. I'm sorry this is going to hurt." She scooped the nearly unconscious woman and slung her over her shoulder.

"The rangers are on the trail," PB said as Violet helped her to stand. "I told them we'd go to the last rented campsite."

"That's three miles." Al adjusted Britt's body with a slight bounce.

"I know," PB said, as she and Violet hop-stepped toward the trail.

"How long until it gets dark?" Violet asked.

PB stared up at the sun in the sky. "Way too soon."

"Focus on the now. We move together, we stay on the trail and we'll get out of here," Alice said.

Violet believed it was possible. She felt the confidence in her team leader's tone but every member was injured—every member was right on the edge of what Violet never expected would be.

The first obstacle was the rocky hill that Violet struggled to climb. She worked hard to keep steady as PB verbally guided them in a zigzag across the larger stones. Alice was faster and pumped with adrenaline that made her forget her own wounds. If anything wanted to track their path out of the forest, Alice and Britt were leaving a bloody trail to follow.

Violet could hear the river water flowing, knew it wasn't far ahead and worried it would be more dangerous now that one of them had a broken leg and the other was half-conscious over Alice's shoulder. "How are we going to cross the river?"

"Two at a time," Alice grunted. She had a plan, and that was all the reassurance Violet needed. "But first, let's get there."

Violet felt Alice's strength like never before. The team leader's knowledge of the park and her experience as a guide were going to help them all survive.

They reached the river close to the crossing point they'd used earlier and Alice laid Britt on the ground. She didn't waste time as she tied her rope to the tree and raced through the water to get across. She was going to do this multiple times so she fastened the line hard. There was nothing fun about this next part; it was life or death.

Alice sloshed back to where Violet waited. She and PB were adjusting the trekking poles stabilizing the broken leg.

"Violet, you and I go first." Alice held out a hand. "You'll need to watch Britt." She pointed at PB. "She's hardly making sounds."

"If she stops breathing, I can't kneel and do CPR with my leg like this." PB dragged herself as close to Britt's unconscious body as possible.

"Do whatever you can." Alice placed Violet's hands on the crossing rope.

"Hurry, Al." PB had two fingers on Britt's neck. "She's so weak."

Al didn't waste a second as she positioned her body behind Violet. "We are going to sidestep together. Left, right," Alice said, and Violet followed the movement.

"Is she going to—" Violet paused as she heard PB yell and shake Britt's shoulders.

"She's got a lot of fight in her." Alice's hands slid beside Violet's, with every pause affirming their connection and giving the two of them strength. The crossing went quickly, but taking Violet would be the easiest trip across.

"I'll bring Britt next. I want her with you and I'm not leaving her alone when I bring PB." Alice grabbed Violet's hands, watching her fear change to confidence. Britt was depending on all of them for survival.

Violet focused on Alice, appreciating on a different level the powerful body she'd desired for the last twelve days. Alice moved like a machine on a mission to accomplish one goal: save everyone on her team.

Britt screamed as Al picked her up and anchored her on her shoulder. Al felt Britt's body weight double as she lost consciousness. Al adjusted her carry,   steadying herself in the water as her back ran against the rope. She used the river's current and the rope to stabilize her and sidestepped, careful to steady herself before rushing another move. It took three times as long to reach Violet.

"Let me help you get her down."

Together, they lowered Britt. Alice didn't pause as she turned to cross the water for PB.

Violet knelt beside the unconscious woman. Her hands roamed the prone body as she checked for a pulse. It was weak, almost impossible to locate, but she was satisfied for now as she tightened the knot around Britt's bundled hand.

The next bit of their route would be the roughest. Violet knew where they had to go—somehow Alice would need to carry Britt down that steep hill. She couldn't manage that incline alone. Violet opened the backpack and dug through until she found the emergency blanket. She searched the riverbank for any material that would make a great support. Waterlogged branches tangled against the shoreline needed to work, and she tucked them in the fabric and bundled Britt inside. It was a makeshift cot, ugly at best but functional with one person at Britt's head and the other at her feet. Together they could share the weight and, with more control, carry her out.

As she finished, Violet looked up to see Alice and PB using one another to stabilize their slippery crossing. It was almost as slow as Britt's, with PB's immobilized leg cutting the water, creating drag Alice had to fight.

PB slipped twice, and each time Alice took the full force of PB's injured body weight. Without the ropes to assist their crossing, all four of them would have fallen in the ice-cold, rapidly moving water.

"Check the splint, please," Alice said as she lowered PB to the ground.

"I swear the water is higher somehow," PB grunted as Violet adjusted the bindings securing the trekking poles in place.

"It probably rained up in the mountains," Alice said. "You do this, Violet?" She was pointing at the material tied around Britt's torso, locking the hand tighter against her body.

"I did. I was thinking you and I might need to carry her down that big hill together." It was a statement more than a question.

"If you get me a walking stick, I can manage," PB interrupted. "And I can scoot on my ass to get to the bottom."

Violet disappeared into the thick tree line, searching for any limb that would make a crutch. She found a perfect branch attached to a tree and tried to bend it over to break it away.

"Here." Alice used her upper body to force the wood to splinter away from the tree. "Use this to cut the splinters." She passed PB's knife to Violet who used the serrated edge as a mini saw blade to cut the limb free.

"Go back to your team," Violet said. She began shaving at the rough cut to make it possible for PB to use. When she returned to camp, PB was drinking water and Britt was too still for the surrounding chaos. The team leader was silent, clutching her hip, and Violet rushed to her side. "Alice," she called.

"I'm fine. I need a moment to catch my breath and then we can go on."

"You're not fine," Violet insisted. She pushed Alice's hands out of her way. "You're bleeding again."

"I know." Alice was covered in her own blood.

Violet unwrapped her hip wound, revealing the fleshy tears and the longest slash. "You need more pressure on this."

"Use the rest of the tape and wrap it tight."

The procedure was ugly as Violet replaced the oozing bandage and proceeded to bind Alice's hip wound over and again, around her back and to the front. It was going to have to work. They were running out of time.

"We have to get moving." Alice grabbed Violet's hands to get her attention. "It's going to be dark soon and with the trail of blood we're making, I don't want the rest of the wildlife following us out."

Violet hadn't considered their safety in the impending darkness or thought about encountering more animals. "Will we make it down that hill in the daylight?"

"Probably not."

Violet turned to help PB stand. "Can you lean on this?" She held the improvised crutch for PB.

"You're an angel, Violet." PB used all of her strength to rise on her good leg and hobble forward. "I'll need some help through the rough spots but I can definitely manage with this." She took the lead position, moving slowly down their trail.

"I'll take Britt's head." Alice gripped the corners of the blanket where they wrapped around the limbs. "You take her feet, and if you get tired, let me know."

Violet wasn't completely sure about this makeshift stretcher or her abilities to carry Britt. As she picked up the corners of her blanket and branch contraption, she looked into Alice's confident eyes.

"We've got this, Violet."

Violet turned to face the trail. She watched PB hobble ahead, making an obvious path to follow. "We've totally got this."

Chapter Twenty-Four

"I'm coming back to help you," Alice said as they passed PB on the trail. The team was less than forty yards from the bottom of the last and biggest hurdle of their escape.

"I'm slow but I'll keep moving," PB said. She'd lowered herself to the ground as the incline became more vertical, and balancing on one leg with her level of pain was nearly blinding.

"How are you feeling?" Alice looked at Violet. They'd switched positions halfway down so Alice could take the heaviest burden of weight on the incline.

"I feel strong"—Violet looked at Britt's face—"but she's so pale."

"She's tough." Alice stepped slowly. "Don't stop moving."

Violet nodded. She did her best to follow each footprint left in the ground by Alice's size-ten boot. Whether intentional or not, Alice's path made for stable ground.

The sun was setting as they reached a place where Alice could lay Britt on the ground. "I'm going back for PB—stay here and put on a headlamp."

Minutes ticked away as Violet watched the trail and felt for a pulse on Britt's throat. The pulse was weak but there, and that was all she could care about as she watched Alice stumble in with PB.

"It fucking hurts," PB said as she was lowered to the ground. "I can't feel my toes anymore."

There was blood on PB's pants, and Alice worried the fracture had broken through her skin. She didn't have time to look or have the emergency kit supplies to treat the wound.

"We have to keep going. Britt hasn't moved much in the last hour," Alice said.

"Is she—?" PB hesitated to ask. She didn't want to give power to the possibility.

"She's alive." Violet nodded. "Her pulse is weak and she's really pale but she's definitely still with us.

"Can you keep walking, PB?" Alice asked as she dug around in the backpack.

"I can do whatever it takes to get out of here."

"Good." Alice slipped the lamp onto PB's head. "Up you go, and let's find the rescue team." She helped her friend to stand.

"Are they coming for us?" Violet asked as she took position near Britt's feet.

"They're coming to the last known location, which is less than a mile from here." They lifted Britt and followed the slow-moving PB. "Don't worry."

"I'm not worried," Violet said but she knew the tone of her voice betrayed her.

"We're getting out of here." Alice paused mid step. Violet felt the pull of the makeshift cot and she looked at her team leader. "We're getting out of here, Violet."

"I believe you."

As they continued, the trail opened into a field. Violet's legs hurt and her arms ached, but there was no way she would complain. She was the least injured of the group.

"You look like you need to stop," Alice said.

"I can keep going." Violet felt the warmth of daylight fading.

"I don't want PB to get too far behind." Alice checked over her shoulder and could no longer see her friend's headlamp.

Violet sat, the darkness kept away by the light strapped to her head. She was feeling the adrenaline rush and her body vibrated from the sensation. She was thinking it couldn't be much longer when she heard a sound from the trail ahead. The tall grasses ruffled and tiny twigs snapped. Something was coming at her, and she was completely defenseless.

"Alice!" Violet screamed, throwing her body over the top of Britt's to protect her from whatever was here. Britt felt cold, but grunted when Violet's weight smashed her injured hand.

Alice and PB were there just before the animal bound through from its position.

"Oh, fuck yeah," PB said as the animal sniffed across Violet's body, barked twice and took off running back the way it came.

Alice dropped to her knees beside Violet who was still laying over Britt. "It's a rescue dog." She touched Violet's shoulder but Violet was frozen to the spot, blacking everything out, prepared to give it all for the injured woman. Alice leaned closer. "Violet, it's a dog."

Violet pushed herself upward, turning toward Alice. "A dog?" she asked. She threw herself into Alice's embrace.

Alice didn't hesitate as her arms came around to hold Violet. She'd wanted this the entire day and needed to feel Violet's heart beating against hers. "You're okay, Vi," Alice whispered as her chin popped the headlamp to the ground. They wouldn't need it now, as she heard the rescue team arrive on scene.

Alice lifted Violet as she stood. Without letting go of the smaller woman, she pointed at Britt's unconscious body. "She's the most injured" was how she greeted the team as she led Violet out of the way so they could work on Britt.

It wasn't cold but she felt Violet tremble against her. When she tried to separate from Violet, the smaller woman held on tight.

"We're safe, now," Alice said over the top of Violet's head, never taking her eyes off Britt and the emergency team's actions.

"Is it just this leg?" a rescue hiker asked PB.

"I'm pretty sure it's come through the skin," she answered, as a second person scooped under PB's arms to set her in a rescue cot.

"We've got three four-wheelers—we can get you all to the landing spot." The rescue team member radioed the evacuation helicopter. "Rescue one, rescue one, ready to extract four to medical transport delta."

Violet didn't know what a delta facility was but she hoped they would get there in time to save Britt and Stacey. She felt Alice's absence immediately as they separated to ride the ATVs. The vehicles were almost as slow as walking as they bounced and bumped into the massive clearing. The helicopter was already on the ground.

Alice knew how to board, so she wrapped an arm around Violet as they crouched beneath the slow-spinning helicopter blades. Alice and Britt had once repelled from a helicopter on a dare. *This ride wasn't any kind of fun,* Alice thought as she sat watching the rescue team secure Britt to the helicopter floor. She wasn't the leader of this team of rescuers so she sat in silence, grateful that the four of them were alive.

Violet leaned into Alice as the helicopter lifted off the ground, relaxing against her. Alice finally had a moment to notice the damage to her hip. She was safe but the sudden knowledge set her fight or flight system into overload as she felt the weight of the day. It was a cougar that tore at her hip. It slashed and ripped at Britt, leaving damage impossible to assess on the trail.

Alice stared at her blood-covered hands. Her body reeked with sweat and the residue of every mile they'd traveled. The water that had soaked through her boots sent a chill through her body, but with every sense of awareness she knew she'd led her team to safety.

The helicopter engine hummed and vibrated, jerking every nerve in Alice's body. As she felt herself drift from reality, Violet's warm body pressed against her tugged her back.

"You did it, Alice," Violet whispered. She knew her team leader couldn't hear over the helicopter noise, but she felt Alice relax as they held each other through the flight.

~~~~~~~~~~

The arrival at the hospital helipad was frenzied as white-coated people yanked at the stretchers. Elevator doors opened, wheelchairs rolled, while Alice and Violet were pulled away from each other.

"What have we got?" the doctor yelled as the team rolled through the emergency room doors one by one.

"Big cat attack," the intern said. She was part of the team transporting PB, Alice and Britt from the helipad on the roof.

"It was a cougar," Alice corrected. "How's Britt?" She tried to get out of the wheelchair to reach her friend. Britt hadn't moved much since the river crossing. She hardly made a sound and the pale color of her face made Alice more concerned than ever.

"They started a line during transport." The intern double-checked the IV and in that same moment the heart-rate monitor set off an alarm.

"We've lost the heartbeat."
~~~~~~~~~~

The world stood still. "Britt, her name is Britt," Alice gasped as each white coat turned toward Britt's bed. Her bloodied hand was the least of their worries. The tallest of the doctors began compressing Britt's chest as they readied the machine to restart her heart.

"Britt is tough, remember." Violet leaned closer, placing a hand on Alice's, having wheeled her chair over to where they were waiting in the hallway.

"She's lost so much blood," Alice said as she clutched Violet's hand tightly. "We weren't fast enough."

"Don't say that." Violet winced as the nurse started to push Britt's chest, forcing her heart to beat. They pressed paddles to her bare skin and the electric current stiffened Britt's body. "We did everything we could."

Alice tried to pull her hand away but Violet squeezed harder. "You did everything—"

"We've got a rhythm," the intern yelled after they shocked her again. At that moment, everything changed. Britt passed them, her body stretched out with tubes and monitors making her unidentifiable to most everyone there. Everyone but Alice.

Alice tried to stand from the wheelchair but when she put weight on the injured leg, it gave way. Her mind wanted to chase after her friend, but her body had other plans.

"Alice!" Violet yelled. The team left behind redirected their attention to the woman on the floor. With the help of two emergency room attendants, they lifted Alice to a bed.

"Can you tell me where you're injured?" the woman in the white coat asked. She noticed Alice was covered in blood and it was impossible to determine the source.

"My right hip." Alice touched the wound and her hand came away red.

"The animal that attacked our friend attacked her too," Violet began. "Alice threw herself at it. Fought it off of Britt."

"It was a big cat—a cougar." Alice tried to sit, eager to know how Britt was and to see PB.

"Lay down." A larger white-coated man forced Alice to stay in place. "We need to take care of your wounds.

Violet watched as they cut away at Alice's clothes, revealing more injuries than previously known.

"This puncture is pretty deep," the doctor continued. "Let's roll her and check the back.

Violet gasped as she saw Alice's bloody clothes fall to the floor. The wheelchair began rolling backward and the curtain fell in front of her face. For the first time in nearly two weeks, the EAG team members were completely separated, and Violet had never felt more alone.

Chapter Twenty-Five

"Can I go in?" Violet asked the nurse as he came out of the hospital room. She'd been discharged hours after their arrival at the hospital, but there was no way she would leave. Her release was simply a formality as her injuries mainly included scratches she'd received during their escape from the forest. She'd gone to the cafeteria for a cup of coffee and some energizing chocolate-covered gummy bears she was planning to sneak to Alice.

"Enter at your own risk," the nurse replied. He tossed the bundle of linens into the soiled bin. "She's the most fun I've had all morning." He snapped the gloves off of each hand and shot them into the waste container. It was obvious he performed this act hundreds of times a day.

"Is she still unhappy about being forced to stay here?" Violet asked.

His lips flattened as he turned to look at the closed door of room two-nineteen. "Unhappy is a kind way to put it." He pushed his cart away from the door and crossed the hall to the next room.

Violet hesitated before knocking three times.

"I'm decent."

Violet pushed the door open, but anchored herself between it and the frame. She didn't know what to anticipate when she walked inside. "Hello, I come bearing gifts." She held up the bag of chocolate candy.

"You can come in, Vi. It's only me in here—finally."

As Violet entered, she was thrown by the sight of Alice appearing less than her burly, independent self in the dress-like hospital gown. The temporary garment looked as stiff and uncomfortable as the woman wearing it.

They stared at one another for a long moment, each assessing the right way to say out loud everything they were feeling.

"Hi," Violet said as tears fell. Her emotions were obvious in the way the word lingered in the space between them. She wanted to climb onto that bed and be held by those strong arms and know that everything they'd endured wouldn't destroy whatever this was between them.

"Hello, Vi," Alice said, and although her voice was low and impaired by the IV drugs, she was solidly still Alice.

Violet pulled a chair across the floor so she could sit beside the bed. It made a loud squeal, startling both of them. Violet looked up into Alice's solemn eyes, witnessing a vulnerability she hadn't seen before. "How are you feeling?"

Alice flipped her gown back, revealing the bandaged wounds. "They're saying I might lose some feeling in my hip."

"Oh, Alice." Violet's heart hurt for the woman in front of her. She knew that Alice would react the second the name came from her lips, but when she did, Violet wasn't surprised.

Alice closed her eyes, tears squeezing from the corners as she struggled to say, "I wasn't sure I'd get to hear you say my name again."

Violet abandoned her chair, left her coffee on the rolling table beside the bag of chocolate-covered gummy bears, and dropped the side rail on the bed. She couldn't bear the sight of Alice, the strong independent force of a woman, falling to pieces in front of her.

Alice shifted herself to make room for the smaller woman and Violet crawled onto the bed. Alice's strong arms came around her as she tucked in tightly against her body.

"I really needed this," Alice whispered across the top of Violet's head. "I needed you."

"Yes, I needed you, too."

They laid together for hours, neither saying a word as their bodies, together, created a sense of certainty they'd found in their tent all those restless nights.

~~~~~~~~~~

The late afternoon sunshine warmed Violet's face. She felt a hand caressing the bare skin on her back beneath her untucked
~~~~~~~~~~

shirt. They'd survived a nightmare of unbelievable proportions. If it was a dream, she didn't want to wake from it.

"Violet," Alice whispered and she squeezed the smaller woman closer.

"Uh-uh, I don't want to be awake yet."

"Vi, you need to wake up."

Violet's first thought was that she had a real nightmare. That she'd fallen asleep in the tent and that no one had been attacked, no one was near death in an operating room, and that Alice was holding her like a lover after their passionate encounter.

But it wasn't so, she realized as the aroma of disinfectant invaded her senses and the beeping of hospital monitors replaced the beating heart beneath her ear. Yes, she was in Alice's arms but they were not in the wilderness. They were in the hospital and although they were safe, they definitely were not sound.

"Vi, a doctor was just here."

That statement got Violet's attention. Her eyes opened to see Alice staring back at her.

"They were?" Her voice was groggy from sleep but she didn't leave Alice's side.

Alice felt the warm breath against the bare skin on her shoulder. The pressure of Violet's body against her had unfastened the snaps while they slept. Alice didn't mind. She needed the closeness of Violet's touch.

Violet's brain processed the context of a doctor visit that wasn't to examine Alice. Her head shot up. "What happened?"

The jolt of her body, and their close contact, shook the bed. Alice felt the pull against her hip and her body flexed from the pain.

"Oh, shit. Did I hurt you?" Violet tried to pull away, desperate to stop hurting the woman who was trying to comfort her.

"I'm fine." Alice adjusted her body so Violet wouldn't leave the bed. "Stay, please."

It was the "please" that made Violet pause—Alice's plea for the same contact Violet also needed.

"Are you sure?"

"Violet, I've never been more certain of anything in my entire life."

"Good," Violet whispered, her eyes closing as she let the invitation sink into her heart. She wanted to stay with Alice, too.

"What did the doctors say?" She sat up, but Alice held tight to keep Violet on the bed with her.

"She was hesitant to give absolutes."

Violet fiddled with the edge of Alice's gown, clearly nervous. "About?"

Alice's words cut through the silence in the room. "Britt's doc was optimistic she wouldn't lose her entire hand."

Violet's body trembled as tears fell. "What else?"

"She'll recover the rest. Most of her injuries are like mine." Alice flipped the blanket from her hip, revealing the gauze covering.

"And Stacey?"

"She's still in surgery," Alice said. "They aren't saying anything else."

"What does that mean?" Violet asked.

Alice lifted her shoulder. She felt helpless tethered to the hospital bed, attached to machines and tubing. She had no control in the situation and she was frustrated by the restrictions. "It means there must be something we missed."

"Stacey had a broken leg," Violet said. "We did what we had to do to get out, that's it."

"There was blood when they loaded her onto the helicopter."

Violet nodded. "The bone broke through her skin."

"We should have—"

"We hiked three miles with Brittney half-alive. Stacey did what she had to do and we will do whatever it takes to help her when all of the dust settles."

"I should have—"

Violet touched her finger to Alice's lips. "Shh, we're alive because of everything you did."

Alice closed her eyes, ready to reject the idea and fight the truth. She felt warm lips against her cheek as Violet shifted close.

"You got us out alive," Violet whispered. "Let me call you my hero for a little while, okay?" She kissed her.

Alice's heart hammered, her pulse raced and the monitor on the side cart began beeping. The door burst open, sucking the tenderness from their intimate moment.

"Inappropriate visitor behavior," the nurse said as he pushed himself between the bed and the monitor.

Violet adjusted her shirt as she slid off the bed. "Sorry," she said, but didn't mean it at all. She was not sorry for holding onto the one person she needed most.

"Your leads came off." He stared at Violet. "I can't imagine how that happened."

Violet and Alice chuckled but the nurse did not as he clipped the wire leads back in place and, with more aggression than necessary, snapped Alice's gown closed.

"Stay off the bed." He pointed at Violet after locking the side rail into the upright position.

Alice laughed.

"You! Don't give me any more trouble."

"Got it," Alice answered, and he left the room.

"Naughty naughty, Violet." Alice knocked the rail with her knuckles.

"I'm not putting that side rail down." Violet fanned defeated hands in front of her. "He's kinda mean."

"That's crap," Alice attempted to roll over to unlock the railing but felt the pull of her stitches. "Fuck. Ouch!" she groaned.

"So damn stubborn." Violet pushed Alice's shoulder. "Keep that up and you're going to be sleeping alone if you make me break the rules." She pushed the button and lowered the rail.

"They won't kick you out." Alice held her arm open. "You're the very best medicine."

Chapter Twenty-Six

Alice and Violet sat in the hospital cafeteria, determining what was next in Alice's recovery process. "You can stay with me," Violet said.

The light in the dining space was brighter than room two-nineteen so they had chosen a cozy corner table farthest from the hustle of the afternoon lunch crowd. Nothing could be quieter than the ICU room they'd just left. PB was in an induced coma while her body fought an infection caused by the open fracture to her leg. This unexpected turn of events left Alice and Britt reeling. Alice ached to hear her speak, even if it was to complain about how terrible the hospital food was.

Britt's flesh and bones were stable for the moment, but Alice needed to know if Britt—the person she loved like a sister—would be the same, and if they could ever return to the life they loved.

It felt selfish to think about the team—about the possibility of hiking and climbing together again. EAG was Al's life, and in the few silent moments of her hospital stay she'd cried over what she was coming to understand would never be the same again.

"Where'd you go?" Violet touched Alice's hand.

Without awareness of the motion, their fingers tangled together. "I'm here."

"Yes, you are."

Alice chuckled as she shook her head. The woman sitting beside her was such a surprise. Violet was released three days earlier but only left her side to wash in the hospital bathroom or check on Britt and PB.

"I said you can stay with me," Violet repeated.

Alice turned to look out the floor-to-ceiling glass wall. The trees were transitioning from green to red and yellow hues, and she thought about her love for hiking this time of year. She ached to be outside. "I can't stay with you."

Violet scooted herself closer to the wheelchair Alice was in. She turned them face to face. "Where are you going to go?"

Alice shook her head. "I don't know."

"Well, see. Now you do." Violet leaned away, crossing her arms over her chest in a gesture that was meant to finalize the decision.

"Just like that?" Alice chuckled.

"Just exactly like that." Vi smiled. "You can't sleep in a tent while you're healing." She waved a hand over Alice's hospital gown covered body. "It could be weeks before you've recovered enough to walk without help."

"Weeks?" Alice frowned. "That's a lot of babysitting."

"Gives me time to work my charms on you."

"Oh yeah?"

Violet smiled. "Definitely."

~~~~~~~~~~~

Al fought an overwhelming need to cry as she opened the door to Britt's room. The monitors pulsed and flicked, reassuring her that the woman inside was alive.

Violet pushed the wheelchair, but Alice stopped it in the doorway with a hand on the wheel.

"Don't be a big baby." Britt forced a chuckle. "Get the hell in here. I'm not dead."

Al released the wheel and Violet pushed them as close to the handrail as possible. Britt sat with her bed upright. Her face was pale and dark patches puffed beneath her eyes. She did not look like the vibrant climber Al had known for most of her life.

"You look like shit." Britt's grin was stunning.

Al looked away. "Aw, fuck you."

"That's more like it."

Violet circled the bed to sit on the opposite side, unsure of her place in their reunion. Britt's body was covered to her hips with a blanket and her injured left hand was immobilized on a foam pad across her chest. Her hospital gown was a perfect match to Alice's, as if they wore some kind of monochromatic uniform for recovery.
~~~~~~~~~~~

Al fiddled with the brake on the wheelchair. "I don't know what to say to you, Britt."

"Just say that no matter what, it doesn't change anything."

Al's head tipped, her eyes wide, and she was quick to say, "Nothing. It changes nothing."

Violet felt like an intruder in the private moment. "I'm going to get some coffee. Can I bring back anything for either of you?"

They looked at Violet, as though they had been unaware that she was in the room. "I'd love a hamburger and fries." Britt pointed to the tray of uneaten food. "They gave me a hockey puck with some kind of yellow glop. I swear they're trying to kill me."

The joke landed flat. "Not funny," Al said.

"Aw, come on. Don't be so serious." Britt stretched to bump her fist on Al's shoulder but couldn't quite reach. Al leaned across to accommodate the ridiculous gesture. "We need to eat."

"Fine, I'll take the same since they delivered that hockey puck crap to me too."

"Great," Violet said. "I'll be back with burgers and fries." She leaned closer to Britt. "I don't know how else to say this but thank you. I don't think I'd be here if you hadn't done what you did." Tears streamed from Violet's eyes.

"I did my job."

"You did more than that," Violet insisted. "And I'll never be able to repay you."

"Bring me a burger and we'll call it even."

Violet forced a smile and brushed her hand across Alice's shoulder, pausing when Alice didn't let go. Their eyes met and countless emotions spilled from that single glance.

"Don't try to do anything without help." Violet squeezed Alice's hand.

"I'm staying right here with her." Alice tilted her head at Britt. "I promise."

Britt snickered like a schoolgirl.

"What?" Alice played dumb but she knew Britt was smart enough to see what was impossible to hide.

"What happened to 'lose her number' etiquette?'" Britt called out the rule that Al was obviously breaking.

Al shrugged. "You've been around her. She's kind of hard to resist."

"I'll be damned if that little powerhouse didn't take out Al Hadley with the flash of dimples?"

"I guess she did."

Britt giggled as she watched Al fight a smile. "So, you and Violet?" For the first time since the attack, Britt's eyes sparkled. Mischief looked good on her and it also changed the energy in the room.

"She's only left the hospital to sneak in food and change her clothes."

Britt tried to adjust her wounded hand but the velcro closure clung to the bedding, piercing the space with a paralyzing ripping sound. "Fuck," she grunted.

"Let me help." Al attempted to stand but felt the pull of her stitches and stapled hip. "Ah, fuck." She lowered herself.

"What a hot mess of a pair we are." Britt laughed as she pried the fabric apart and the ripping sound of velcro made them jump again.

"I can't believe it, Britt." Al picked at the rolled edge of her gown.

"Sometimes things happen," Britt said. "But we're alive."

"It happened so fast." Al's voice hitched. "And I didn't know how to save all of you at once."

"The only thing we could do was exactly what we did," Britt said with no regret in her voice. "You fought a goddamn cougar and won."

Al stared at the immobilizer attached to her best friend. "Your hand didn't. I don't know what to say to you."

"Stop being the boss for a minute." Britt's head fell back against her pillow. "We have to slow down and give it time. We don't know enough yet and we won't know for months what my recovery is going to look like." She shifted her elbow to flex her immobilized hand.

"I couldn't fix them," Alice whispered. "They were gone."

"It doesn't matter." Britt struggled to continue. "The doc says there was too much time between the severing to even attempt reattaching them. The risk of infection was too high, considering I nearly died. It must have been pretty gruesome all over the forest."

Alice looked into serious hazel eyes. "There was so much blood."

"You saved my life." Britt closed her eyes, unable to fight the emotions she'd smothered for days. "I don't know how I'll ever be able to repay that debt."

Watching her friend and hearing the humble, tear-filled decree made it impossible to fight the tears any longer. Al's body trembled. "There's no debt. I only want you to be here."

~~~~~~~~~~

"They're letting me go home." Alice crossed her leg in front of the other to lean on her crutches. "My discharge is dependent on home care and daily revisits to begin rehabilitation therapy. So I can stop by and see you whenever I want."

"Are you living in a hotel?" Britt pushed the button on her bed to raise it to the highest seated position. The velcro on the foam support beneath her hand tore loudly and the two of them froze.

"Fuck that sound," Alice whispered as she shifted her weight on the crutches. Violet was hiring a car to pick her up and she needed to reassure Britt she wouldn't be alone.

"Yeah, maybe I can request less velcro." Britt repeated her unanswered question. "Did you get a hotel?"

"No, not a hotel." Al swallowed hard. "I'm going to be staying with Violet."

"Oh. My. God!" Britt laughed as she poked at her friend. "You're getting it on with her, aren't you?"

"What are you, five?" Al shook her head.

Britt slapped the bed. "No, I'm eight." She wriggled her fingers and pointed at her bundled hand.

"That's a terrible joke," Al said.

"Maybe, but don't change the subject. Are you and the worst knot tyer in the world doing it?"

"We aren't doing anything with this." Al rotated so that her body was closer for Britt to see. "My hip is a hot mess, so nothing is going to happen."

"But something did, didn't it?"

Al placed her crutches together and leaned against the bed. She wasn't going to try and sit, but she also wanted Britt to be the only one to hear. "She's not the person I thought she was."

"You judged her based on one shitty skill."
~~~~~~~~~~

"Life-saving skill, it turns out," Al said without thinking. "Sorry." She looked at Britt's immobile arm.

"No, it's true. Some things take time." Britt was about to share wisdom acquired in the dark nights trapped inside her hospital room. "I'm not going to let this stop me."

Al nodded.

"I'm going to get out of here and get my ass right back on the trail." Britt's lip trembled as she added, "I don't know how to do anything else."

"Remember, I'll be right beside you."

Britt struggled to wipe her tears on the shoulder of her gown. "I'm counting on that."

Chapter Twenty-Seven

Violet woke in the middle of the night to the sound of Alice's scream. She watched in horror as the woman fought the space between reality and dreaming. The bed they shared was large enough for two but not terribly comfortable when Alice still needed help with mobility.

Violet's house was a modest, single-story fixer-upper, but it was hers. When she invited Alice to stay, she had every intention that they would share a bed, but in her haste to bring comfort she couldn't have predicted how intense Alice's nightmares would become.

"Alice?" Violet hesitated to touch her. The light of the moon from the picture window cast wild shadows.

"I'm okay." Alice's voice was rough as she held her hip, trying to separate the physical pain from the emotional darkness of her dream.

Violet rolled closer. "You're not okay."

"I'll be fine." Alice held up her hand. "Just go back to sleep."

There was nowhere for Violet to go and no way she could turn her back when she heard the fragile sound of Alice's muffled sobs. Violet closed the space between them, pulling the blanket away so their bodies could touch.

"You don't want to do this." Alice's shoulders tensed. "I never should have come to stay here," she whispered as she flexed to move away. She couldn't let Violet take on more, knowing that if she did, all the delicately woven threads of the last few weeks would unravel and the truth of her pain would be impossible to hide.

"Alice." The whisper felt like a caress.

"Please, Vi." This was the make-or-break moment of Alice's life—the truest test of courage as she trusted Violet's ability to catch her as she fell.

A hand touched her cheek. "Please what?" Violet asked.

"Please don't." Alice sobbed.

"Please don't what?" Violet persisted.

"I'm falling apart. Don't be so wonderful when all I can offer you is this mess that I am."

Violet pressed her palm against the mattress, hovering close enough to see Alice's tear-filled eyes. "I'm not being wonderful. I'm being concerned."

"You shouldn't."

"You just said you're falling apart."

"I know," Alice whispered.

"I'm not trying to fix you." Violet wiped the tear on Alice's cheek. "All I want to do is be here and maybe, if you'll let me, I can take care of you."

Alice's voice hitched. "That's all?"

Violet's lips paused a breath away. "And maybe if you stop talking, I might want to kiss you." She smiled.

"Only a kiss?"

"For now," Violet whispered.

Alice placed a hand to cover her forehead, protecting herself from a potential bump.

Violet smirked. "Seriously?"

"I don't think I can handle another injury."

Violet took Alice's hand, tucking it between them. "I'm not going to hurt you." Their lips touched, featherlight.

Alice felt less like the clumsy kisser who'd nearly knocked them out in the forest.

"Okay?" Violet asked.

"Very okay." Alice let out a slow breath. "Very okay, for now."

Violet was careful as she moved against Alice's uninjured side, hesitating as she tried to discern where she should place her hand.

Alice solved the dilemma, as her fingers tangled with Violet's and fell against her abdomen. Her heart raced, and she wondered if Violet could feel it where their bodies touched. There was lust, and longing, but above all there was fear of loss like never before. Violet was the kind of woman Alice would change her life to love.

Violet settled in, her soothing voice breaking Alice from her inner struggle. "It sounded like a pretty bad dream?"

"Mm-hmm." Alice didn't want to share the details, knowing the truth would scare the woman in her arms.

"Do you want to talk about it?" Violet asked. Her arm tightened around Alice before she could pull away. Alice was predictable—her shoulder stiffened. "Stay right here," Violet demanded. "You can say yes or you can say no, but you're not going to put walls between us and you're definitely not running away."

Alice pushed the mattress to leverage her hip. It was enough to prove to Violet that she could run if she wanted to, but that she was staying because of what she saw when Violet looked into her eyes. "You're scrappier than I thought you were."

The moonlight lit the room as Violet turned to look at Alice, and she knew that if they fought through this trauma they would be alright. "I stood up to you, didn't I?"

Alice nodded. "You amaze me, you know."

"You kind of amaze me, too." Violet leaned in for another kiss, this one less tentative but equally soft as they touched. She held herself closer and smiled. "I'm guessing you don't want to talk about it?"

Alice chuckled. "Will you shut up if I do?"

"Shut up?" Violet was offended.

"Be quiet?" Alice raised her eyebrow, questioning if the adjustment would fix the misspoken phrase.

"Be quiet?" Violet scoffed at the suggestion.

"Oh my gosh, woman. Would you let me rest if I tell you I can't stop seeing everything covered in red?"

Violet sat up. "What do you mean, seeing red?" She pulled the blanket off to look at the wound on Alice's hip.

Alice pressed her hands to the bed again; the only way she could move her hip without pain was to lift the dead weight. "My wound is fine. It's Britt. I keep seeing Britt."

"Oh." Violet's response was barely a whisper. "I should have known."

"How could you?" Alice fell back against the bed.

"I see her, too, but I'm hanging above you all and I'm safe. I couldn't move. I could only watch that animal tear into all of you."

"I'd do it again."

Violet pushed the sweat-soaked hair from Alice's forehead. "I know you would." She kissed her tear-stained cheek. "That's one reason I'm here."

"I killed that animal with a hunting knife." Alice held her palms out. "With my bare hands."

"I saw it all." Violet caressed her callouses.

"I can't stop reliving it." Alice sobbed in Violet's arms. "I'm not sure I'll ever be the same."

"I don't think any of us will."

~~~~~~~~~~

Alice ended the call from the hospital. "That was exhausting." She was sitting in Violet's kitchen, with her bare feet pulled up onto the seat. It had been over a month since the attack and the pain of her injury had faded into scars on her body and her soul. As she healed physically, several wounds from the puncture site had little to no feeling. If the lack of sensation was the main long-term result, Alice believed she could live with the loss.

Violet stood at the cooktop, heating soup for lunch. "What did they have to say? How's Stacey?"

As Britt's hospital care had been extended and the therapies had progressed, one thing had become clear—the injuries to her hand were permanent but they no longer threatened her life. She'd been released and had moved across the country to stay with her half-sister. It wasn't ideal for Alice's need to see her, but Britt's sister was there with love and emotional support to help her through the physical therapy ahead.

What had come as a surprise was the extent of PB's injuries and the complications from surgical malpractice.

"PB needs another surgery. This will be the third time they open her up. There's another infection growing from the placement of the metal rod," Alice explained. "She's so ready to get out of the extended care medical facility she's in."

Violet set the bowls of soup on the table along with a plate of grilled-cheese sandwiches. Cooking wasn't a strength of hers,
~~~~~~~~~~

but they were making it work. "It must feel like jail, if she's anything like you. The same way that you were ready to escape?"

Alice waved a hand to scoop the scent toward her nose. "It was more stressful to be in that hospital than anywhere I've ever been."

Violet sat across the table from her. "I'm glad you didn't feel that way about coming here."

Alice raised a spoonful of soup and blew across to cool it down. "Thank you for inviting me and for all the rest." She smiled as the flavor touched her tongue.

"Can we talk about all of the rest?" Violet dunked the tip of her triangle-cut sandwich into the soup.

"I might need a few minutes." Alice watched Violet bite her sandwich and grin with pleasure from the taste.

Violet finished chewing before saying, "I'll give you three minutes."

"That's not a very long time," Alice argued.

"Maybe not, but there are things that you need to talk about and if you can't do it with someone who was there, you need to find someone who wasn't." Violet set the sandwich on her plate and noted the time. They sat together, not speaking a word, with the ticking of the clock the only sound, as three minutes passed like days.

"You know, I love your arms around me when we sleep, but the nightmares are getting worse, not better."

"I can manage them," Alice interrupted.

Violet pushed her bowl away. "I know that this is new—whatever this is between us—but lies will always kill a relationship."

"Lies?"

"You're lying to yourself if you think you can get through what happened to us on your own."

"I've made it this far."

"Have you?" Violet questioned her. "Sweat-soaked nightmares is 'making it' through?"

"I need time." Alice said.

"Yes, we all do but it's more than time," Violet said.

"So what is it?"

"It's us, going through life and death and not pretending it was a minor stumble."

Alice's hands rubbed the surface of the table. "You're infuriating."

"You've said that before." Violet ate a spoonful of soup as she watched Alice sort her feelings. This wasn't their first disagreement about emotional care and she was sure it wouldn't be their last.

"Why?" Alice asked.

"Why, what?"

"Why are you still here?"

"Because it's my house, Alice," Violet said.

Alice pushed away from the table. "You know what I mean." She picked up the bowl and plate.

"I do know, but why won't you say it?" Violet put her hand on Alice's arm. "After everything we've been through, do I really have to answer that question?"

Alice studied Violet's features: her frown, the confusion in her eyes. She knew disappointment when it was looking at her and she didn't want Violet to look at her that way. "I don't want you to have to go through whatever comes after all of this." She patted her hip.

Violet stood, the weight of her full five foot, three inches planted firmly in Alice's path. "Will you believe me when I tell you I want to be here and that I want to be here with you?"

"Why?"

Violet shook her head. "You're the infuriating one."

Alice crossed her arms. "Maybe I am."

"Right now, there's no maybe about it."

Alice hobbled to place her dish in the sink. "I need to take a walk."

Violet stood, realizing in that moment that Alice didn't need her help. "Your cane is by the door."

Alice stopped in the archway that separated the kitchen from the living room. Her fingertips hooked over the heavy wooden trim, and the grip felt familiar. She closed her eyes, delighting in the comfort of that finger-grip muscle memory. She wanted more than anything to raise her feet, challenging the strength of her core and, more importantly, flex the skillfully-stitched repair to her hip, but she didn't. *Healing takes time*, she thought, and Violet was on her side for the physical part and the mental.

Violet watched, unsure what was happening as Alice's hands dropped and she turned around.

"Walk with me?" Alice held out her hand.

Violet took hold of her hand, tipping up on her toes as she kissed Alice. "I was hoping you'd ask."

Chapter Twenty-Eight

Violet leaned close to whisper in Alice's ear, "You're like a little kid."

Alice was bouncing in her seat as they rode in the taxi from Violet's house to the storage facility where Bess had been moved less than a month earlier.

"I wonder if they kept her cover on." Alice tipped her head toward the window as they turned into the parking lot.

"You covered her?" Violet chuckled.

"Of course I covered her. I was going to be gone for two weeks." Alice started to open the car door before the taxi came to a complete stop.

"Hey, you gotta wait 'til I park," he yelled.

"She's a little excited." Violet read the meter on the dashboard and paid the driver.

"Yeah, well, she needs to wait, next time."

Violet opened her door and double-stepped to follow Alice, knowing the driver was right but also giving leeway to the woman stabbing her cane against the asphalt and limping as fast as she could to get to her car.

Three hours earlier, the doctor had cleared Alice for all activity including moderate climbs and driving. That was all she needed to hear, and before they went anywhere else, she'd called for a taxi to take her to the short-term storage facility.

Violet waited outside the office as Alice spoke to the reception clerk. Her cane was hooked over the edge of the countertop as she explained her limp and the need for a cane. The clerk handed her an envelope along with a hot-pink wooden spoon.

Violet was extremely curious about the spoon. "What's with that?" she asked as Alice stepped out of the office.

"The spoon?" Alice shuffled the envelope to her cane hand. "It's for the gate." She waved it in the air. "It keeps people from driving away with it, I guess."

"Funny." Violet chuckled as she increased her pace. Alice was obviously in a hurry as she keyed the lock and pushed the sliding gate aside. "Where is she?"

"That's the cool thing. The owner heard about the accident and he parked her inside." Alice followed the signs on the doors. "We're looking for six eighty-eight."

Violet checked the numbers painted on the ground. "It looks like we need to go down that row." She pointed toward the criss-crossing intersection inside the gated facility.

Alice checked the crude sketch on the back of the envelope. "Great sense of direction." She kissed Violet. "I'm so glad you came along."

"Are you kidding?" Violet smiled. "And miss my chance to witness the reunion between you and your first love?"

"Britt." Alice shook her head. "I can't believe she did that to you."

"She was vetting me." Violet's dimples appeared.

"Was she?" Alice contemplated the revelation.

Violet tucked her hand in her pocket, checking for the surprise she had for Alice. "She definitely was."

"It doesn't feel right to call her my bitch anymore."

"She'd probably hate it if you stopped."

"Maybe." Alice paused in front of unit number six eighty-eight.

"You didn't say much about your call with Britt this morning," Violet said. She was patient when it came to discussing the team members' recoveries. She knew that Britt was spending more time in therapy than either of them, and her progress was slow. PB's transfer to a new facility brought lawyers into the mix as everyone was ordered to stop communicating with the original surgeon. There was talk about amputation before a second opinion uncovered that critical mistakes had been made.

Of the three team members, Alice was making quick progress physically, but they had yet to come together in the same place at the same time. Alice wanted that more than anything.

"She's frustrated," Alice said. "Worried about PB, and mad. She's so mad."

Violet wrapped an arm around Alice's waist. "I think all of those feelings are normal."

Alice squeezed the hand on her waist. "Yeah, but—"

"It's going to take time."

"The three of us aren't very good at being still." Alice leaned her cane against the wall of the storage unit.

"That is the understatement of the year." Violet's hand fell away. "Are you going to open it?"

"I don't know why I'm so nervous." Alice fit the key into the lock and slid the door across the track. "Aw, they kept her covered."

"The cover kinda adds to the drama," Violet said. "It's like you're giving me a big reveal."

"It is." Alice circled around to pull the cover off the back bumper.

"Can I help?" Violet asked.

Alice raised a halting palm. "No, stay right there so you can really feel the magic."

Violet thought it was charming, like a proud parent introducing their firstborn child.

Alice balled the cover under her arm as she returned to Violet's side. "What do you think?"

Violet noticed one thing first and got down on a knee, a curious look as she recited the license plate. "One M B three five S." She grinned at Alice. "Did you plan it like that?"

"Nope, and Britt was the one who noticed it right away."

"She would." Violet's finger danced over the hood, traveling along the decorative pinstripe that went from front to back. Alice delighted in Violet's enthusiasm.

"So, this is your girlfriend, Bess?" Violet teased.

Alice shook her head. "Bess is not my girlfriend. Remember I don't have one?"

Violet scoffed. "Are you sure you don't?"

Alice's eyes widened as she realized what was happening. "Do I?"

Violet took the balled-up cover from beneath Alice's arm. "I think maybe you do." She flashed her dimpled smile.

Alice cupped Violet's cheek. "How would you feel if I did?"

"I'd feel like you should take me for a ride so I can get to know your first love a little better." She tipped up on her toes, moving closer for a kiss.

"Size up the competition?" Alice kissed her.

With hooded eyes, Violet whispered, "Something like that."

Alice led her girlfriend to the passenger side, unlocked the door and helped her in. As she walked around the front of Bess, she smiled. Violet was caressing the dash and speaking to the car. Her first and last love was definitely in this storage unit.

Alice tucked her cane in the back seat and threaded herself cautiously in the driver's seat. Aside from a bit of dust, Bess looked the same. She still had hints of the new-car smell, and sitting in the driver's seat righted a few tilted angles of Alice's jumbled world. She felt for the key.

"Wait," Violet whispered. "I have something for you, and for Bess, too." She reached in her pocket and held up a shiny red stone dangling from a chain. "Happy birthday."

"You remembered." Alice chuckled.

"I know your birthday is a few days away, so maybe it's also for a new beginning."

"A new beginning. I like that." Alice tapped the rock with her fingertip. "Is that the one you found in the river?"

"The red rock that stumped you, yep." Violet took Alice's hand and placed the keychain in it. "I'd say it's a very lucky rock."

"Maybe it is."

"Do you like it?" Violet asked.

"Chicks dig red, don't they?"

Violet chuckled. "I supposed some do."

Alice threaded the chain onto her keyring. "This chick does, for sure." The stone jangled against the steering column as she keyed the ignition.

Violet stared out the windshield, the monotonous slatted metal doors the only thing she could see, and for some reason the moment felt right. "I'm in love with you, Al."

Alice's hand froze as she turned toward Violet. "What?"

Violet sat, her hands in her lap, smiling innocently as if she hadn't just blown Alice's mind. "I said I'm in love with you."

"I heard that part." Alice's hip pinched as she turned in her seat. "You called me Al."

"I wanted to get your attention."

Alice shook her head. "By calling me a name that we fought over?"

"Mm-hmm." Violet was suddenly serious. "I wanted to be sure you'd hear me the first time I told you that I love you," she whispered. "I'm in love with you."

Alice closed her eyes. "I'm in love with you, too."

"I know." Violet smiled.

"You know?"

"I saw it that day when you covered me with your body and stayed all the way down the rock wall," Violet explained. "And I felt it when you touched me by the river." Her cheeks flushed. "Because, sweetheart, when you show your emotions, they're impossible to miss."

"Just to summarize, you're saying you love me?" Alice started Bess's engine.

"That's what I said, and what I meant." Violet laid her open palm on Alice's thigh.

Alice swiped the tear on her cheek. "Not a lot of people say that to me." She shifted the car into drive and took hold of Violet's offered hand.

"That's about to change."

"I see that."

Violet chuckled. "It's about time."

Alice exited the car long enough to secure the storage-unit door and returned to the car. She maneuvered to the exit and waited for the traffic to pass. "Where to?"

"Are you up for a long drive?" Violet asked.

"I might be." Alice smiled.

"How'd you like to meet my aunt Eunice?"

Alice turned onto the highway. "I'd actually love to meet her." She adjusted her hip, feeling a prodding in her lower back.

"Are you okay?" Violet asked.

Alice pulled the bright pink item from behind her. "I can't believe I almost forgot the spoon." She reversed into the parking lot, carried the huge pink spoon to the office and returned before Violet could offer to help. They paused at the gate. "Where do we go from here?" she asked.

"Wherever you want."

Alice laughed. "No. I mean, which way to your aunt's house?"

Violet's dimpled smile was accented by embarrassed rosy red cheeks. "East," she said.

"East it is." Alice signaled her direction and zippered onto the highway.

Violet turned her back to the passenger door, staring for a silent moment as she gathered the courage to repeat Alice's question. "Where *do* we go from here?"

Alice held out her open palm to the smaller woman. "Wherever you lead, I'll follow."

"Really?" Violet was surprised that her team leader would acquiesce so easily.

"Okay, I'll mostly follow."

"Mostly?" Violet questioned.

"Occasionally. I'll occasionally follow."

Violet held the offered hand. "That sounds more like the Alice I love."

"I like the sound of that." Alice kissed Violet's hand and tucked it to her hip.

"Yeah, I like it too."

The End

Double Dyno

If you'd like to read more of their story. You can find Alice and Violet living happily ever after, mostly, in Yule Be Home For Solstice.

More Books from the Author

<u>Rage Room Romance Series</u>

Book 1
CONNED

For Ella Eastman, firefighting is life. She's devoted her body to being the best, but everyone needs a break from reality once in a while. For Morgan Hail, art is life, but she has to make a living. Their lives collide when television fandoms intersect at The Blacktree Comic Palooza.

Morgan's captivating fanart leads to a heated misunderstanding, and a cosplay contest brings these two women together–though only one of them knows the truth. This unlikely pair heats up when their real-world lives collide, but what will happen to their budding romance when Ella reveals her secret identity? And can they find a way to make things work when Ella's job hits a little too close to home? Conned is a story of love, loss, new beginnings, and fandom.

Book 2:
DECONSTRUCTED

After eight years, Ella Eastman has a plan to create the perfect marriage proposal for her partner, Morgan. Inspired by Morgan's to-be-read pile, Ella struggles to incorporate her favorite romance tropes while asking the big question. The ideas pile up, as do the failed attempts to create their once-in-a-lifetime memory. How do you give the perfect partner the perfect memory of a perfect proposal? For Ella, it all seems to come together quite imperfectly. Revisit the Rage Room Romance's chosen family as they unite for Operation Perfect Proposal.

THE LEGACY OF THE MAKER
(BOOK 4 OF THE MAKER SERIES)

In a secret world filled with magick, Wildwood Blackstone has encountered unbelievable mysteries. As the blacksmith in her new hometown, she's survived and endured the call to wield the hammer of the goddess Brigid, but to what end?

Celebrating a year with her girlfriend, Shay, the two continue their search for answers. What lived inside Andrea Peters? How did the entity survive for hundreds of years? Who controlled her all this time?

Their call to be The Magick and The Maker of Bannock comes with more questions than ever, but it might also come with answers to their past. Wildwood and Shay are drawn into endless realms, all of which lead to the Legacy of the Maker.

BEHIND THE EYES

Theirs was a love story for the ages: Rasabel, the captain of the guard, and Isolde, the woman of the territory. In a world of swords and arrows, love could not defend against a cruel curse. For years, they searched for an end.

When the alarm bells of Acadia ring, Rasabel goes home, but she is not welcome. Her path collides with Bylyn, a young thief on the run from the executioner's axe. Their lives are forever entangled.

Can Rasabel and Isolde find hope in the hands of a girl who will do anything to keep her freedom?

DEAR KANE;
WHAT I WISH WE WOULD HAVE SAID

Do the words that we say in front of our children build them up or tear them down? This short story explores the consequences of hatred and bigotry when it applies, unknowingly, to someone that you love. There's a time in every relationship when a parent must let go of the dreams they have for their child, so the child can chase what they dream to become.

IMMORTAL HUMAN TRUTH

Immortal Human Truth is a collection of poetry written by the author as she traveled to promote her first book
Dear Kane; What I wish we would have said.
Each section explores experiences with love, injustice, loss, and triumph of the spirit.

SHE BELIEVED SHE COULD

What can you do in a single day? Why haven't you done it yet? Jump out of your comfort zone and dive into life as you follow the author on her journey to achieve 365 new experiences in 365 days.

ABOUT THE AUTHOR

Sharon K. Angelici, she/her, was born in the American Midwest, but her heart and soul belong to the mountains of Colorado.

She began writing as a child, using words to recover from trauma-induced depression. As a member of the LGBTQ+ community, she's an advocate for depression awareness and suicide prevention. In 2016 she published her first book dealing with both subjects, *Dear Kane; what I wish we would have said.*

Sharon is a full-time lover of life and all things Pagan and Magick. She's an artist and blacksmith, which inspired her to create her Maker series.